"Weesht!" hushed his father as the voice of Neville Chamberlain came over the radio.

First published in 2000 by
ABERDEEN ENVIRONMENTAL EDUCATION CENTRE
Top Floor, Skene Square School,
61 Skene Square, Aberdeen, AB25 2UN.
Tel: 01224 640864
Fax: 01224 639626
email: aeec@cwcom.net
www.aeec.mcmail.com

British Library Cataloguing in Publication Data
A catalogue record for this book is available from the British Library

ISBN 0 9539064-0-X

Cover design by George Galbraith
Printed and bound by Nevisprint Ltd.

Watt Mitchell

Shepy's War and Peace

With illustrations by
George Galbraith

Aberdeen City Council

Aberdeen Environmental Education Centre

Aberdeen Environmental Education Centre

Preface

Aberdeen Environmental Education Centre is part of the Services to Schools and Centres section of Aberdeen City Council's Education Department.

Through work with pupils, particularly in primary schools, the Centre promotes environmental education in the curriculum with an emphasis on devising first hand experiences in the environment. These learning opportunities provide a strong stimulus to further investigation back in the classroom. Through direct contact with the environment, pupils become aware of the problems that confront the environment today. They are encouraged to think about their role in preventing further damage to an already stressed environment. Resources focus on the environment from several perspectives including geographical, historical, scientific and the natural sciences.

Our resources support the 5-14 curriculum, in particular environmental studies, and are used in many parts of Scotland.

Shepy's War and Peace

Individual behaviour is determined, in part, by attitudes prevalent in society. What has come before has shaped the environment we live in today. There are many lessons to be learned.

Shepy's War and Peace contains valuable insights into the recent past and into the culture of the North-east.

Acknowledgements

Here is a collection of stories for young and old, about boys: boys fighting, boys playing, boys at school and even boys in love, but written with humour and just a little pathos. Most of them appeared in the Evening Express during the early Eighties.

Watt Mitchell was born (1930) and brought up in Aberdeen and educated at local Skene Street, Rosemount and Central schools.

Most of his working life has been in the printing world, where he worked as a compositor, Monotype operator and proof reader with Aberdeen University Press and Aberdeen Journals. Latterly he was a storeman with oil company Total. As a freelance writer he has had many articles and features published locally.

Front cover artwork and story illustrations are the work of George Galbraith. Although not from the Aberdeen area, George was enthralled by the stories. They struck a chord with his own experiences and sense of humour. He met and got to know the author, Jack Irvine, before finally deciding on the most appropriate style for drawings. The result is a collection of illustrations which adds a visual dimension and so emphasise memorable moments.

George Galbraith was born in Belfast in 1953, and studied art in Kent and London, where he trained to be a teacher. He taught and practised as an artist in Scotland for 10 years, before moving to Bournemouth. He is married, with two (artistic) children.

Introduction

The war brought grief and tragedy to many. As one of Scotland's most bombed cities, Aberdeen had her moments. Happily, most children survived unscathed. Certainly Shepy wasn't bothered. It just never occurred to him that Britain could lose the war.

There were minor irritations with imported fruit, including oranges and bananas, disappearing from the shops, ice cream discontinued, sweet rationing and a scarcity of toys. But there were compensations: lessons interrupted by air raid warnings; salvage collections; backyard concerts and shrapnel souvenirs. Shepy made the best of things, taking every day as a new adventure.

Contents

Page numbers

Through the eyes of a child

SHEPY awoke with a groan. It was Sunday and again he was confined to the house – as far as getting out to play was concerned, that is.

The previous day, neighbour Mrs Hutcheon complained about him kicking her Robert, returning from the Regent Cinema Saturday morning Mickey Mouse club.

"Fitiver gart ye kick 'im in the stamack?" his mother tackled him reproachfully.

"It wis his ain fault," reasoned Shepy with his own brand of logic. "He shouldna've turnt roon."

The smell of bacon, eggs and fried bread wafted through to the bedroom. He forgot his predicament for the moment. Breakfast was always late on a Sunday. Lunch, at what he knew as 'dennar time', was thus saved on.

The main meal would be taken between 5 and 6pm at what they called supper time. Having snatched a few hours sleep after a 9pm to 6am night shift, Shepy's father was focusing bleary eyes on his favourite Sunday paper, Reynold's News.

Just through the letter box from Cheyne's on Leadside, it was full of the steady drift towards war.

Later on, a three-way swap with mother-in-law and brother-in-law in the same tenement yielded Empire News and Sunday Dispatch.

Now up and dressed, Shepy expected his breakfast. However a pound note was thrust in his hand to get tea, cocoa, 10 Woodbine and a cake of chocolate (for afters) from Cusiter's, just along the road and always open on Sundays.

A talk on making the most of tinned food was on the radio as he prepared to go. It reminded Shepy of being sent just recently with tins of food to a lorry in the street, collecting on behalf of the Popular Front in the Spanish civil war.

"Dinna lose the change noo" his mother shouted after him as his thoughts drifted to the young brother of a next door neighbour.

A *beau sabreur* in Shepy's book, in an act both heroic and tragic he had volunteered for the International Brigade and been killed in Catalonia for his efforts.

This was an issue about which Shepy knew his father felt strongly, to the point of wishing he was single so he could go and fight Franco. In his first steady job for some time, however, he opted to stay put and look after his family.

When Shepy returned from Cusiter's, his parents were waiting intently for the broadcast and paid him scant attention.

Depositing the purchases in his mother's lap, Shepy handed her the change declaring: "It wis jist two an' six a'thigither. At's siventeen an' six back."

"Weesht!" hushed his father as the voice of Neville Chamberlain came over the radio.

"I am speaking to you from the Cabinet Room at No. 10 Downing Street." The premier sounded very old, tired and sad.

Rising slowly, Shepy's mother deposited the errands on the table, retaining the packet of Brooke Bond tea. She stepped towards the fireplace, her attention divided between the beehive-shaped Ultra bakelite wireless set on the sideboard and the willow-patterned tin tea caddy on the mantelpiece.

"...unless the British Government heard from them by 11 o'clock that they were prepared at once to withdraw their troops from Poland, a state of war between us ..."

Tearing open the packet, she emptied it carefully into the caddy and replaced the lid before crumpling up the wrapper in her hand and tossing it into the fire.

"... I have to tell you now that no such undertaking has been received, and that consequently this country is at war with Germany."

Shepy brightened. He reckoned troops would be marching off to war down Union Street right away, led by brass bands, like in films of the Great War. He would surely get out now.

"It's jist as weel ye collected the ARP photies," he enthused, referring to the well-known Air Raid Precaution cigarette card hints, as his father lit a cigarette from the green and brown Woodbine packet on the table.

The grim look on his father's face as the prime minister laboured on shut him up, however.

In cinemas, Shepy had seen for himself newsreels of German and Italian bombing in Spain. He was aware Germany had overrun Austria and Czechoslovakia. Now they had invaded Poland and he felt only a surge of excitement as he listened to the broadcast.

"May God bless you all. May he defend the right, for it is evil things that we shall be fighting against – brute force, bad faith, injustice, oppression and persecution; and against them I am certain that the right will prevail."

Although the news was hardly unexpected, there was a stunned silence for a few seconds as the gravity of the situation sank in.

It was broken simultaneously by the National Anthem and Shepy's mother.

She held out a hand containing three silver coins. "Hey! Faur's the rest o' my change?" She looked askant. "There's only seven an' six here!"

Shepy, mouth full, almost choked with indignation. "I gave y' it," he spluttered. "I gave ye back siventeen an six."

Looking at the three half crowns in her hand, his mother then gazed with tragic intensity at the coal fire blazing in the grate. It dawned on her what she had done.

"Oh my God!" she gasped. "I've thrown a ten bob note up the lum with the wrapper!"

For the moment the National Anthem went unheeded. Neville Chamberlain was forgotten, Adolf Hitler was not even considered and the fact that we were now at war with Germany was almost irrelevant.

A ten shilling note (50p), almost 25% of the breadwinner's wage had gone up in flames. This was a tragedy, no mistaking. Certainly more immediate than a far off war which would take some time to be felt by Shepy's family.

But, as sure as night follows day, felt it would be in many ways: danger, discomfort, disappointment and deprivation, by people of their ilk the length and breadth of the land in the months and years which lay ahead.

Fleein' Freddy dispenses the runs

ON LEADSIDE, right in the middle of the road opposite Strachan's Mill at the top of Jack's Brae stood a police box. Timber built, maroon painted, with a Georgian hipped roof, the "bobbie's hoosie", a familiar landmark, was surrounded by sandbags.

Huddled inside the cramped quarters, Shepy and his pals awaited their fate. Their crime? Playing in the underground air raid shelters in the Grammar School. Despondent, they sat on a bench comforted only by the last of the chocolate squares they had been sucking incessantly during the day.

That morning on his rowie delivery run up Rosemount, Smike's wee brother, known as Fleein' Freddy because of the speed he did his round, spotted double tablet chocolate samples on doormats in Wallfield and had gathered up all he could lay his hands on. At home, he stripped off the covering, popped the squares into a paper bag and had been sharing them all day with his sweet-tooth chums.

This was not the first time they had been in trouble, not their first time in the "bobbie's hoosie". They had long since outgrown the petty offence of ringing doorbells and running away.

Their last escapade of that nature had been smoking out auld miser Simpson in Mackie Place. Gaining access to the roof of his house from a wall on ground at a higher level, an ample sod was placed across his chimney with mischievous delight.

Since then, the occasional broken window or pane of glass in a lamp post, invariably caused by football in the street, brought them wrong side of the law in the shape of "Slicer", otherwise known as PC Slessor.

To avoid playing in the street, they used the Grammar School Westfield playground, revelling in the green-painted pillars supporting the roof of the bicycle shed as goal posts. But this haven too, was out of bounds.

The construction of underground air raid shelters in the Grammar School grounds was a Godsend to kids in Northfield and Leadside.

Anderson shelters, sunk into the ground, were confined and often flooded. Brick and concrete-made surface shelters were cold, dark, damp and stank!

Roaming through the maze of well-kept underground passages, scarcely illuminated by bulkhead caged lights on the walls was thrilling enough. Every blast-proof section of tunnelling had a bucket latrine

and wooden steps leading up to a large metal grating which could be raised; slightly, to pinpoint the whereabouts of the janitor if he was on the prowl or pushed open completely, as a means of escape.

For an hour or two, they wandered undisturbed through the tortuous labyrinth of corridors, chasing each other, playing hide and seek or engaging in make-believe battles. If they kept their heads down, chances of discovery were slim. But rushing out and in the entrances was asking for trouble. Thus it was the janitor spotted them.

Then things became really exciting. As the janitor gave chase into one entrance, they would lead him a dance, pop out another, waving and pulling faces at their tormented hunter.

Reinforcements arrived and caution was called for. But there were still too many exits for two janitors to cope.

Over confidence was their undoing. Ascertaining the bearings of both janitors, they made a dash for the Carden exit and ran full tilt into the waiting arms of "Slicer" and a newly-enrolled special constable.

Now sitting disconsolately awaiting the return of the policemen, deliberately confined as a punishment and kept in doubt as to their destiny, Shepy felt tummy pains. The others were experiencing similar uncomfortable symptoms.

When PC Slessor at long last reappeared, they were looking pretty wretched and woebegone, wincing and writhing about, suffering stomach spasms and cramp.

"You little rascals are nae tryin' it on are ye?" cross-examined the suspicious constable, viewing them with mounting disquiet.

Freddy was examining a sample wrapping he'd kept in his pocket. The dubious policeman grabbed it. Almost immediately, he slapped his thigh and laughed uproariously.

"Gweed God! Hiv ye bin eatin' 'at?" he guffawed. "Brooklax! Ye've a' bin takin' laxative!"

Mindful of the inadequacy of the sole "watery" on the premises, before the purgative began to act, he hurriedly added "Ye better a' get goin' richt noo."

Pushing open the door he hustled them out, fairly certain they would be out of circulation for the immediate future. Due to Fleein' Freddy's faux pas, they most surely would be on the run for a day or two, but at least it would not be from the long arm of the law.

All is revealed

... she looked aghast at the intruder, her eyes like saucers.

SHEPY'S bedroom was last to be done. Three-inch-wide strips of black-out paper were pasted round the window, and a large screen of cardboard tacked to a flimsy wooden frame was lifted into place. A far cry from early days when an old bed quilt showing light through the threadbare patches had been pinned up, but still a lot cheaper than the heavy black-out material costing about two shillings a yard.

"The toon cooncil say we're saving £70 a nicht in street lichting as a result o' the black-oot," Shepy's mother quoted from the Evening Express.

Optimists forecast, despite official talk of a two-year war, that it would be all over by Christmas and that a permanent black-out was a waste of time and money. Now doing fire-watching and ARP duties at the Infirmary, Shepy's father had learned the hard way that brown paper tended to tear when put up and taken down daily, and drawing pins pressed into the same holes night after night ceased to grip.

The activity in progress was enjoyed by Shepy although his role amounted to little more than fetching and carrying and switching on and off the light for his father. In any case, he was about to set off to his pal's house at the other end of the street, so it was as well that his father's task was completed.

"Hiv ye deen a' yer home work?" asked his mother.

"Aye."

"Weel, be hame by half-past nine, ye hear?"

He nodded. The black-out posed few problems for Shepy. He'd got acclimatised to prowling about the darkened streets with his pals, easily avoiding the innumerable hazards, like kerbs, lamp posts, pillar-boxes and sandbags piled high outside the old fish shop, now a police and ARP warden post and scarcely visible in the inky blackness.

"Pit oot that licht!" was a familiar cry as the black-out was vigorously enforced on householders by police and wardens. Fines of 5 or 10 shillings were levied for showing a light. A magistrate fined a soldier £1 for striking a match in the street during a raid, and some members of the public would denounce their neighbours.

Guy Fawke's night was ruled out for the duration. And a game of "I spy with my little eye something beginning with ..." was a non-starter. No longer were shop windows aglow with light in the dark evenings.

Anyone who did not experience the total blackness of those wartime nights would be hard put to grasp the sense of isolation and near panic if one lost one's way. In most streets the only light was the pin-prick glimmer from the cut-out cross on the shielded lamp-posts.

Shepy and Eddie Munro were bosom pals. The Munros were Catholics, but Skene Street school goalkeeper Eddie was an avid Rangers supporter, idolising their 'keeper Jerry Dawson. From a non-religious Protestant family, Shepy was a Celtic fan with winger Jimmy Delaney his footballing hero.

Heavy curtains were drawn and, in homage to the black-out, a cardboard shade made from a cake box was placed round the light bulb over the living-room table in Eddie's house. It created a gloomy impression in the room, but this was lost on four budding capitalists grouped round the table playing a brand new game from the States called Monopoly.

And thus it was for a couple of hours or more, Shepy was absorbed in buying and selling, renting and trading, with Eddie, his brother Norman and Eric Smith, known as Smikes, who had brought along the expensive game, each trying to bring financial ruin on the others.

It was considerably later than they had promised their parents when Shepy and Smikes left the Munro household.

Half-way along the road, Smikes said his goodbyes and, Monopoly box tucked under one arm, disappeared into the entrance to his tenement to tackle six flights of stairs to the top floor. Shepy, happily flushed with his efforts as a financier, veered diagonally across the road in a bee-line for his door.

When he hit the lamp-post he was in mid-stride and caught it, like a sledge-hammer, full-face. He didn't fall, but reeled back dazed and disorientated and unsteady on his feet. A shooting pain and flashing lights, surely defying the black-out, exploded between his smarting eyes, and his nose ached and throbbed unbearably. He felt sick and very foolish.

Clasping a hand over his face as if to soothe the stinging pain, he staggered the last few yards to the door.

Hands still shading his pulsating profile, Shepy tottered into the living-room and heaved a sigh. Squinting through parted finger, he meant to make the most of his mishap so his latecoming might be overlooked. He was not, however, prepared for the sight that met his sore eyes.

A few years older than Shepy, Nessie Campbell, was no Venus, but she was a very big girl. Standing naked in a three foot tin bath on the hearthrug, plump posterior warming in front of the coal fire, she looked aghast at the intruder, her eyes like saucers.

Transfixed to the spot, injuries momentarily forgotten, sheer curiosity delayed Shepy's astonished, lingering eyes meeting hers. Contact prompted a scream from the exposed girl that could be heard in Jack's Brae.

The black-out was to become a classic excuse for many minor misadventures. But Shepy's uncharacteristic blunder into the wrong tenement through a genuine mistake was most surely a brief initiation in the opposite sex – an eye-opener, in fact!

Gutser wins trench coat warfare

At once his arm shot up above his head.

HIS brand new dark gaberdine trench coat had gone. It certainly was not hanging where he left it that morning. Panic stricken he scuttled through the other "pegs" making certain he wasn't mistaken, but all that was visible was an abandoned balaclava and mangy scarf.

Worn for the first time, purchased from Duncan Fraser's Schoolhill drapery for 24 shillings and sixpence plus 11 clothing coupons, the light rain shower that Monday morning had decided his mother.

"Ye micht as weel weer it. At's fit it wis bocht for," she pronounced. "But for heaven's sake tak' care an' nae mak' a sotter o't the first day oot!"

Running downstairs at the playtime interval, in the usual pushing and elbowing stampede to get out first, Jocky Norrie, a pasty-faced, runny-nosed kid also known as Bubbly Jock because of the frequent patch of green mucus at his nose, aimed a kick at the seat of Shepy's pants, catching him instead in the small of the back, causing him to fall, skin his knees and elbows and get a bump on the head.

In the tussle that followed, rolling about on the ground, Shepy gradually wrestled Norrie face down, sat on his back and twisted his arm.

Now, stunned, he just didn't know what to do. Everyone had gone, including his pal Eddie Munro who was always "dying of hunger" at this time. He would just have to go home alone, coatless and face the music.

It was to be upsides with Eddie Munro that he had got the coat. His chum always wore good quality clothes. Shepy's poor mother knew – he told her often enough – that Eddie had not only a trench coat, but a nap coat, a kilt and brogue shoes.

There was no hope of competing on that level. Clothing coupons were a great leveller – a good excuse if you had no money. Some folk had cash but lacked coupons, but many had more coupons to spare than cash. Eddie's father enjoyed regular work as a baker, so fortunately the Munros could afford to use up their clothing coupon allocation.

Shepy dreaded going home bearing the bad tidings. It was dinner time and he hadn't even managed to hold on to his new coat for the first half of the day. And little sympathy for his injuries was forthcoming when his mother learned he was minus his new coat.

"Fit? Ye've lost yer spleet new coat?" she exploded. "How could ye dae sic' a thing?" Shepy had scant enthusiasm for his dinner as his overwrought mother ranted and raved on. But when she declared her intention of accompanying him back to school to get to the bottom of it, he almost choked. That was the very last thing he wanted, but he was powerless to stop her.

A strict disciplinarian, Miss Ironside ('Irongutser' to the kids) spared no one. Boys and girls were strapped with equal vigour if they had it coming to them. As a consequence of her firm rule a great deal of fine teaching was accomplished.

Her prune face creased with displeasure and distaste as she listened intently to Shepy's mother.

Later, when all were seated, she grimly faced her class and asked if anyone had taken the coat by mistake or otherwise. There was no response.

"Does anyone know anything about the whereabouts of this coat?" she asked. "Think carefully children. I may have to inform the police."

That did it. After a long, pregnant pause, Dod Doig's hand shot up. "Please, miss, it wis Jocky Norrie fa teen it!" he blurted out.

"I saw him as weel, miss!" seconded Andy Jamieson dutifully.

Miss Ironside directed a baleful, intimidating glare towards the wretched Norrie.

"Well boy?" she boomed. "What have you to say for yourself? And blow that nose of yours at once!"

"No, miss. It wisna me, miss. Onywye I didna ken it wis his coat," he bleated. "I didna mean tae tak' it."

Now floundering and at a total loss, a pained expression appeared on his face and he began to snivel.

"Well ... he shouldna've twisted my airm. It's awfa sair," he blubbered. "It feels as if there's a burning dagger in it." He proceeded to nurse his arm, grimacing and wincing for effect. "Look, miss. I canna hardly lift it."

Having immediately and most sternly dealt with and disposed of all needful arrangements concerning the return of Shepy's trench coat, it was quite some time later before the resolute teacher once more surveyed her pupils. Pursing her lips thoughtfully, Miss Ironside actually appeared to soften.

"About this aching arm of yours, Norrie," she said gently, "show me just how high you can lift it."

After a great show of physical effort combined with pained facial expressions the ingenuous Norrie slowly raised his arm just shoulder high.

"Now," the shrewd primary mistress encouraged sympathetically, "show me how high you could lift it before the injury."

At once his arm shot up above his head.

Irongutser sighed as she reached into her drawer for the strap. Sore arm or not, Jocky Norrie was about to pay for his crude, vengeful transgression with a belting from Skene Street School's champion "scudder".

In a cellar under the stairs

ALL of them heard the siren. Shepy and his family had become quite accustomed to its unmelodious, undulating wail as a matter of fact. And like a lot of other people they chose to ignore it and take their chances with the Luftwaffe.

At school next day, Shepy and children of families reacting in the same way would no doubt jeer at those who had got out of bed apparently unnecessarily to take shelter. Surely it was obvious to everyone by now that it would be just another false alarm.

So the explosion really took them by surprise. It didn't sound far off either. The whole tenement seemed to shake on its foundations. Also badly shaken were Shepy and his family.

There was no denying that things had been very quiet. Apart from a few sorties with trawlers at sea and some tip and run raids along the coast there had been months of comparative peace. Several nuisance alerts, yes, but they had all come to nought. Phoney war, they said. But something was definitely happening now!

"Aneith the table! Ca' canny! Watch yer heids!"

Leaping from the kitchen bed recess Shepy's father, galvanised into wakefulness, grabbed his trousers and confronted his children who rushed frightened from their rooms to their parents' bedside. Hurriedly he gathered and bundled them with their mother under the kitchen table in the centre of the room and crouched there apprehensive, arms stretched out protectively, awaiting the worst.

On shift work and with a part-time evening job when shifts allowed, he put his sleep before "social gatherings" down in the cellar, which he considered a waste of time. His family, believing he knew best, followed his lead, although Shepy's mother had misgivings about this attitude to the alerts.

"C'mon. Intae the lobby. Double quick!"

Overhead the drone of bombers could still be heard as Shepy's father hustled his family into that confined space in the flat where all doors met, reckoning it might be just a little safer there. In that postage-stamp spot, surrounded by doors to kitchen cum living room, bedrooms and lobby press, they huddled together shivering in their pyjamas.

Shepy's father was feeling somewhat guilty. He knew he'd been wrong exposing his family to great risk. But his actions were being repeated all over the city. It was early days in the war with much, much worse to come. People had yet to learn that in the hundreds of air raid warnings there would be less than three dozen actual bomb attacks. But which would be strikes and where? That was the question. The only answer was to take shelter each and every time.

Regular concrete or under ground shelters in backyards, school playgrounds and parks were as yet few on the ground and people living in tenements would flee to the cellars below ground level carrying their gas masks just in case.

Some people dreaded sheltering in basements, believing everything would collapse in the basement, burying them. In a house in King Street one woman refused to accompany her family to the basement, claiming she was safer where she was. When the all clear sounded and her family were coming in the door, the back boiler blew out, killing instantly the unfortunate woman.

Mind you the cellar under the stairs in the depths of Shepy's four-storey tenement contained a variety of worn armchairs, kitchen seats, deck chairs and an old couch arranged in a cosy semi-circle with a small kist of drawers for a table and old rugs on the floor. Some of the furniture had been stored there since before the war, but was now being put to good use. The ground level window was blacked out and a couple of candles afforded the only light.

Things had by now gone quiet. The dust had settled as it were and Shepy's father decided they should collect their clothes and make a dash for the cellar. Opening the door they streamed down two flights of stairs to the ground floor past the buckets of sand on the landing, down the back stairs, then through the door leading to the cellar and finally down steep wooden steps to the dim lit vault below the house.

All the tenants were there by this time. The genteel Gregories with young Bertie; the easy-going Farquharsons and children Freda and Ernie; middle-aged Paterson the market gardener and his wife Bella; the shop owners Keith with grown daughters Betty and Nellie; widower printer Mr. Charles and grown daughter Ina; Shepy's uncle George and aunt Alice with little daughter Sheila; his Granny with her daughter Nan and husband George, plus his own parents and two younger sisters.

There was not a great deal to do except talk. The weak light made reading difficult but the women could sew or knit. Occasionally there was a sing-song and tea from flasks. The men would play cards, tell jokes or congregate on the back porch steps, scanning the skies, in company with search light beams, for signs of intruders.

For emergencies a chamber pot was a must and Shepy's uncle George always the joker, had painted the interior of one with Hitler's face adding the caption "Adolf in Po-land". Anyone requiring the facility couldn't ask for a better target!

The long distinct strain of the all clear sounded. Everyone cheered up and relaxed. Shepy could now go to school an hour later than usual.

Visibly relieved, Shepy's father had learnt a lesson. But he wasn't one to dwell on it. With a 6am morning work start clearly on his mind he aimed to salvage what he could of his night's sleep. He fixed his sleepy family with a wily grin.

"Fit aboot us a' gaun back tae wir scratchers richt noo? Eh? Fa'll be first ane hame – aifter me!" Then he was off leading the way up the cellar steps, his children scrambling eagerly behind him.

Waiting in the wings

THERE, IN the wings offstage in Skene Square School, all made-up and swathed in emerald green garb with Robin Hood cap, Shepy stood petrified. Stage fright, sheer panic, blind terror – he suffered the lot as his heart went bump, bump, bump.

Unwisely, he had taken a peak through the curtains, seen the large audience and become completely overwhelmed by the whole business. The cue was getting nearer, but he knew he would not be able to go on.

First night nerves? This was the only night!

What had started Shepy in this sort of caper was his parents' insistence on his sister and him doing a turn at weddings and parties. His father could sing a bit and his efforts – "*When day is done*" and "*Goodbye*" – from the White Horse Inn always went down well.

At sing-songs around the fireside his mother would harmonise as they all joined in favourites "*With someone like you*", "*It's only a shanty in old shanty town*", and "*Just a song at twilight*". Or they would accompany the gramophone 78's of Richard Crooks, Grace Moore, Arthur Tracy, Frank Crumit, Layton and Johnstone, bought every other week from Paterson, Sons & Marr Wood or Neil & Co. in Queen Street at two or three shillings a time.

Shepy's party piece was "*Smile awhile*" while his sister trilled:

"*I'm a merry little mandarin*
From a flowery land I come.
I sailed across the China Seas
And my name is Chum Yum Yum ..."

Then along came the backyard concerts as part of the war effort, and Northfield tenements hosted open air evening recitals on the drying green. Enthusiastic tenants and neighbours sat on the porch steps, adjoining walls, even the wash-house roof, watching the performers – mostly kids.

Delectably attired little Marie Clark brought the house down with her rendering of "*Sweet little Alice blue gown*". Pretty Alice and Pearl Reid did a credible impersonation of the Andrews Sisters and Doris Pyper, Audrey Kelman and Shepy's sister tickled the spectators with their bubbly spirit.

David Glass played the mouth organ and Bob Insch was a dab hand with spoons. Nevertheless, outnumbered among the girls and ribbed by his pals, Shepy judiciously switched to plaintive cowboy songs. "*The last round-up*," "*The wheel of the wagon is broken*," "*The last of the Texas Rangers*" and one spelling it out more prophetic than he realised:

"*I'm a-ridin' down an unknown trail*
Where I'm headin' for there aint no knowin' "

The driving force behind the concerts was a selfless, go-ahead woman in Esslemont Avenue. Yes, Mrs Coull saw to just about everything and, while the top-notch little band she mustered played gems like "*Near you*" and "*Sweet Sue*" she was mindful of talent suitable for bigger performances she staged.

Incredibly, Shepy was recruited. Mrs Coull rigged him out in a cowboy outfit, stuck a stringless guitar in his hands and got him to warble hillbilly ballads "*Darling Nellie Grey*" "*Old Faithful*" and "*Goodbye Daddy darlin'* ".

It was one thing out on the grass at the back of the house. He was now up in front of a lot of people on proper seats, even though they were mainly proud mothers, dutiful aunts and doting grandmothers.

Finishing with a hat-doffing flourish he was staggered by tumultuous applause

Rehearsals began for a grand concert in Skene Square School, boasting a large hall and stage, where the audience would be augmented by servicemen and women. Not exactly enamoured with his new role, Shepy acquiesced when promised a western encore.

Now his big moment had come and he couldn't face up to it. All prompting behind the scenes was to no avail. He had completely dried up.

Suddenly Mrs Coull gave Shepy a vigorous push on to the stage. The band immediately struck up. The crowd cheered. Shepy was momentarily blinded by the footlights but, like clockwork, went through the various steps and routines he had practised, simultaneously bouncing about the stage and belting out his new number.

"*There's a little devil dancing*
In your laughing Irish eyes ..."

It was frightening to go on stage but there was no stopping him now. Switched on, brimming with vitality, confidence growing with each verse, he was now thoroughly enjoying himself and a new sense of power.

Finishing with a hat-doffing flourish, he was staggered by the tumultuous applause. Breathless, he took several theatrical bows before being whisked off.

"Fit aboot mi uncore?" he protested vehemently.

"Later," he was assured.

Turn after turn went on. Kitted for his cowboy part he waited hopefully in the wings, desperate for a few more moments of celebrity. But it was not to be. There were many more acts and too little time for the stage brush encore which, in part, reflected his disappointment.

"*Now I'm lost and forlorn,*
Wish I'd never been born,
Since they cut down the old pine tree."

Unfortunately, impresarios Emile Littler and Val Parnell missed the proceedings. The band broke up soon after as members were sucked into the armed forces.

Looking after two nephews and a niece – orphaned in the Clydebank blitz – kept Mrs Coull and her gardener husband very busy, and thus ended Shepy's bid for stardom.

Riches of a ragman

"HIVYE ony rags yer throwin' oot missus?" inquired Shepy, stretching wide the faded old bolster before the woman who answered the door. The stock reply, "I'm weerin' 'em a' laddie," made him groan inwardly at its repetition, but he would grin hugely as if hearing an inspired flash of wit for the first time. This time the answer was promising.

"Hing on a minitie. I micht hae a pucklie fer ye." Shepy leaned back on the banisters. There was little doubt in his mind. He was on the road to a small fortune.

All week in school he'd been thinking of it as Miss Ironside droned on about the curly hair of sheep from the temperate grasslands with almost half the world's yield from countries of the British Empire, whereas the vegetable fibre cotton was produced on sub-tropical grasslands with the USA in the forefront.

Now, systematically, he covered the whole street, from top to bottom of each tenement, counting on his newspaper round customers, at least, to contribute something for his pains. It was, after all, part of the war effort. When a mere two ounces of knitting wool cost a clothing coupon, it was just his good luck that the going rate for woollen rags was 9d per lb.

As a wee kid he could remember hearing the discordant blasts on a battered bugle heralding the arrival in the street of the ragman. Within minutes he would join the swarm of children coming from all directions bearing rags of every description to be exchanged for goldfish, celluloid windmills, bubble pipes or colourful balloons festooning the ragman's cart.

Beyond that stage now and unlikely to be fobbed off with childish trinkets, Shepy was aiming for a bigger prize. The progression to his present way of thinking had, of course, been gradual and had begun years earlier.

One of a small band of young children under the leadership of an older youth – Moshie Morrison, dubbed king o' the kids – Shepy took part in expeditions up the virtually adjacent west end scraunin' the backets, an exercise which was more or less a crude form of salvage.

Rich indeed, at times, were the pickings with delights like the ramshackle typewriter which nevertheless worked, an ancient gramophone complete with giant horn and sound box, a rattletrap racing bike still roadworthy, rickety golf clubs, plus the usual assortment of defective metal toys, tattered books, cracked golfballs and erstwhile gimcrackery.

It goes without saying that Moshie collared the pick of the spoils, but each member of the gang ultimately got something – no one left empty-handed.

Utilising a set of time-worn camera lenses rescued from a Beechgrove bucket and a cardboard shoe box, Shepy's uncle George made him a magic lantern which projected magnified pictures on the wall. And the spoked wheels from a rusty old pram sentenced for scrap up Wallfield way formed the basis of his cairtie, now given a new lease of life and pressed into active service in salvage drives.

It was now big time. The calls were for waste paper, aluminium pots and pans, kettles, tins, bottles and jam jars, gramophone records, bones, films, rags, lino, tyres – and children joined enthusiastically in the national campaign for salvage.

Ornamental iron railings disappeared from house gardens in Whitehall, Belgrave and Esslemont Avenue, and from the Victoria and Westburn parks as their removal became compulsory. Church and cemetery gates were not spared and in some cases the chains and railings around graves were removed.

Shepy and his pals plumped for waste paper. The shortage of paper was very serious. Newspapers were reduced to four pages and many magazines and well-loved children's comics disappeared entirely. Among Shepy's favourites, first the Gem and then the Magnet and Skipper boys' papers were victims.

Out came the fleet of cairties and they combed the streets in the neighbourhood gathering all the papers and periodicals they could lay their hands on before trailing the lot round to Henry Munro's waste paper depot in Little Chapel Street.

Queuing with kids from the Viaduct, Denburn, Gilcomstoun and Leadside, they were rewarded with one shilling per hundredweight. Mind you, before it weighed that amount the folded papers were piled higher than Shepy. It was money well earned.

Collecting rags was not nearly so hard, and he was getting something from most doors he knocked on. Cast-off smocks, frocks, jerseys, flannels, bloomers, semmits and mittens all helped to swell his capacious bolster.

"Ye maun hae a pun' or twa there," commented old McArthur at the foot of the street sizing up the contents as he stuffed a holey sweater and threadbare combinations into the well-filled bolster. "Och, I'll

"I'll gie ye half-a-croon fer the hale lot," he growled.

wight there's a stane in there."

"Na," corrected Shepy, "there's naethin' bit rags." The old gentleman gave him a merciful look, slowly shook his head, then grunted, "Aye. That'll be richt."

Small street depots handling scrap materials were numerous, but Shepy's destination was a recently established rag merchant in Farmers' Hall. With a sense of eager anticipation, Shepy proudly dumped his bulging bag by the scales in the untidy little yard.

The thickset, bald-headed dealer immediately shook out the contents and speedily separated them into two piles, one larger than the other. He weighed each heap, muttering away to himself. Finally, he straightened up, turned to Shepy and flung the empty bolster back at him.

"I'll gie ye half-a-croon fer the hale lot," he growled.

Shepy was dumfounded. "Fit? A' that and only half-a-croon?" he complained. "I thocht it wise ninepence the pound." The dealer glowered impatiently. "Look at the boord!" he bawled. "Pure white wool 9d per lb. OK? A'thin else tippence ha'penny. Nae muckel worsit there, maistly linen or cotton.

"Oh. I didnae ken it wis jist wool ..." Shepy faltered, crestfallen.

"Well, ye ken noo!" scoffed the merchant with not an ounce of kindness.

Somewhat chastened, Shepy turned for home. Collecting rags wasn't what it was cracked up to be. Maybe the dealer cheated a bit, but if he'd done less wool-gathering in school he might have understood wool's standing among other fibres.

Lady's choice

"He-e-y-y, Lady" yelled Shepy watching her rapid disappearance...

"HEY fit aboot gyaun tae the Links wi' us tae look fer shrapnel an'at." Shepy was out in the street exercising the dog when he met up with Sandy Insch and his genial older brother Bob. They crouched and began to stroke and fondle the animal in friendly fashion.

Looking on proudly, for he loved his pet immensely, Shepy was sorely tempted to take up their offer. Searching likely areas for German bomb shrapnel, anti-aircraft shell splinters and spent machine gun cartridges was a popular past time.

Living a couple of streets away in Kintore Place, Ginger Cruden returning home had been hit in the leg by a German plane strafing Rosemount and had the bullets to prove it in his collection. Normally, Shepy would have had no hesitation. Now, however, he seemed uncertain.

"Nah, I dinna think so," he replied ruefully. "I'm nae supposed tae ging too far awa wi Lena – I mean Lady – ye ken." The tan collie at his feet was not the only dog to figure in Shepy's thinking, which accounted for his aberrant reference to Lena.

A long-legged scraggy, scrawny mongrel, with a black coat and too long tail, Lena belonged to the easy-going Polsons just along the road and was the friendliest creature you could meet.

Endearingly clumsy, playful and wildly enthusiastic as a pup, trying to lick you to death, she learned to put up with the more often boisterous than affectionate maulings of the kids in the street.

By comparison, Lady was just that. A well-proportioned, refined, reddish-gold Shetland collie, whose sensitive, intelligent behaviour earned her respect and admiration. She could also be pensive and aloof at times, making Shepy feel she took him for little more than a stripling.

Unfortunately, the kids began to tease Lena unmercifully. From a tenement doorway they would shout the dog's name, bringing her careering down the street only to have the door slammed shut in her face at the last moment. Leaping over the backie walls they emerged from a door farther along the road and did the same again. The exercise was repeated over and over until they were exhausted and the poor dog demented.

No such treatment befell Lady who several months, earlier had trailed Shepy's father home all the way from the Infirmary despite attempts to elude her and stern commands for her to go home. On the doorstep a last stand was made.

"Shoo! Gwa hame!" he gesticulated. "At's a gweed doggie noo. Gwa hame!" Hearing the commotion Shepy's mother appeared.

"Fit's adee?" she queried. "Fit's a' the steer aboot?"

"Weel it's jist some dog 'at winna ging awa!"

"Mercy be here," she pouted, opening the door wide. "The peer wee craitur'll be stairvin'." Feeding the dog in wartime was no easy matter. Lady, as she became named, had arrived. And as the days went by she gradually became their dog and was loved as one of the family.

Meanwhile, Lena was fast becoming a nuisance, charging about the street and gardens in a state of perpetual excitement, running circles round people, yapping and jumping up at them. Worse, she began chasing and challenging cars, lorries and cyclists.

For a dog it all comes down to one simple thing: Love for its master, and there was no mistaking Lady's allegiance. A soft whistle or gentle call from Shepy's father would bring her instantly to his side no matter what she was doing, and she ran to him when he came home, yelping joyous greeting. Shepy envied his dad's mastery.

When his father was on awkward hospital shifts, Shepy was entrusted to take her but advised to go 'jist doon the brae or roon the squaries'. The one bordered by Northfield, Esslemont Avenue and Leadside was actually a triangle, adjacent to the longer route taking in the Viaduct and Skene Street. Right now he swithered.

"Aw c'mon, ye'll be a richt," Sandy reassured him with an appealing grin. "Bob'll be wi's us a' the time." It was true that things were rarely dull when Sandy's gung-ho brother was around, so Shepy swithered no longer and Lady padded along dutifully by his side as they set off.

Threading their way down the myriad of streets on the walk to the Beach, Shepy recalled the shock he received that fateful night returning with Smikes from the Life Boys in Correction Wynd. It was his best pal Eddie Munro in Cub Scout uniform looking very agitated.

"Hiv ye heard aboot Lena?" he accosted them excitedly. Apparently up to her usual tricks, this time harrying a cyclist near the notorious blind spot where Northfield crossed Leadside, the mongrel was in mid bark when the front bumper of an army truck clipped her head and shoulders, sending the poor brute spinning into the side of the road and out of this world.

Shepy knew the kids in the street were really to blame for Lena's sad end. Uneasy feelings of his own guilt bothered him. Calling Lady to heel, he determined to never let that happen to her. But events beyond his ken were about to take hand.

They had skirted Queens Links, keeping clear of barbed wire areas out of bounds and were near the bandstand when the wail of a siren signalled an air alert. Lady pricked up her ears, turning her head to listen gravely and looking up at him with her intelligent eyes. A decision was made there and then to head for home.

Suddenly, the air was rent by an earth shattering noise as the anti-aircraft rocket launchers beneath the Broad Hill let loose a ferocious barrage. Simultaneously, the ack-ack batteries at Balgownie and Balnagask opened up.

The boys were startled, but none more so than Lady who raced off in the direction of Urquhart Road as if struck by lightning.

"He-e-y-y, Lady" yelled Shepy watching her rapid disappearance into the distance with dismay. "Come back! Come back!" But the collie was gone.

Convinced that she would not have fled in his father's care, Shepy was as inconsolable as his father was compassionate.

That night and the following days and weeks Lady's absence filled the house. Perhaps she found her rightful home. Perhaps a new home. But they never saw her again.

Requiem for a soccer tenderfoot

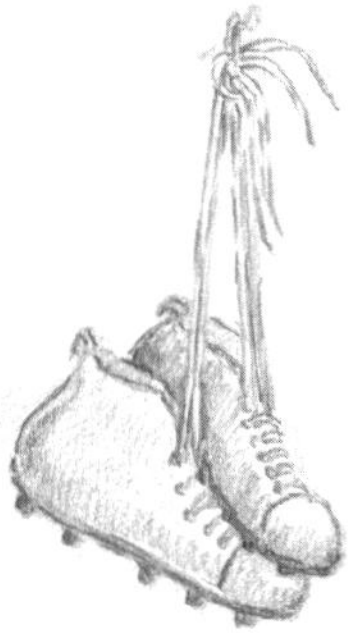

"*ALL men must be free.*
Fight for liberty with me."
Shepy delivered the rousing words to Elgar's strident battle anthem with great gusto as Mr. Henry, zealously accompanying the class on piano, beamed approvingly.

Rapport you could call it. It didn't happen often, but Shepy appeared to hit it off with the music teacher from the start.

What really cemented the bond was Shepy's vocal enthusiasm for the patriotic music Mr. Henry favoured.

Hitler's armies had seized no less than 14 countries and driven deep into Russia. But Britain no longer stood alone and, galvanised by the earnest music master's morale-boosting choruses, it was difficult to feel down-hearted. So Shepy let himself go, belting out the Soldiers Chorus from Faust and was promptly earmarked for the school choir.

No such concord was in evidence with register teacher "Fatty Corker" later that day as he delivered a rebuke on the prevalent, despicable practice of deflating teachers' bicycle tyres, threatening to strap the entire class should no one own up.

The corpulent English teacher, who closely resembled Dracula horror movie actor Bela Lugosi, had a unique way of strapping pupils.

Wrongdoers were made to place their hand, palm upward, on his desk. Anyone moving his hand sideways to evade the descending tawse was subjected to a flurry of savage swipes.

"This tiresome behaviour must cease," he lectured solemnly. The class erupted at the deliberate pun. But it was no laughing matter when he commenced "scudding" each boy in turn as promised, since no culprit was forthcoming.

Equally ebullient, but with a wry grin apparently permanently locked into his tanned countenance, was the wisecracking, enthusiastic Mr. McKenzie, known as "Kenzer" the teacher who most won Shepy's respect.

Kenzer's quick-witted mocking repartee deterred most pupils from testing his authority, and those foolhardy enough were soon tamed by the tall, tough maths/science master.

Presently in the boys first year class A at Rosemount School, having overcome dismay that most of his Skene Street pals were in class B, Shepy was due to transfer to the Central School in six month's time.

"Kenzer", whose greatest dislike was idleness, spent much of his time after school hours coaching and preparing Shepy and kids from Skene Square and Mile End schools – a function little appreciated by the struggling schoolboys he was trying to help.

As sports master, his pride and joy was the football team. Some new players would be recruited from the January intake and in the Probables versus Possibles trial Shepy gave a reasonable account of himself.

"And as for you, I'd have been a damn sight better leaving you with the choir!"

When the team for Saturday was announced Shepy could scarcely believe he'd been picked, the only one from class A to get in the team. Several players were provided by class B, lending strength to the view that the less academic are superior at sport.

In the playground he burst into song in sheer delight at his lot:

"*And ready to fight,*
And ready to die
For good old Rosemount!"

Then it struck him. The school choir and his obligation to Mr. Henry. The events clashed. In the science room he unburdened his dilemma to his new mentor.

"Just you leave it to me. I'll see to it," grinned Kenzer conspiratorially, much to Shepy's relief.

Shepy was intrigued the day before the game to spot an item in the Weekly News about veteran Rangers' defender Duggie Gray whose speciality was performing spectacular goal-line clearances.

After reading the story several times he was so impressed by the international full-back's technique he determined to adopt for himself this line of defence.

Well, the day dawned, the match got under way and Shepy certainly kicked and headed several balls off the line, but more often got in the way of agile goalie Alex Hay!

In taking out of context one particular strong point in the famous ex-Aberdeen Mugiemoss player's armoury the absurd plan was doomed to failure. Instead of marking and tackling opponents Shepy lingered in the goalmouth playing them onside and allowing shots at goal.

Tricky winger Johnny Bain scored early on but the final result – Middle School 5, Rosemount 1 made Kenzer livid. Stamping about Harlaw pavilion, face purple, he was at his brilliant best lampooning the team. Bain should have been "left outside"; Hay would be better taking up net ball.

Towering over dejected Shepy, he shrivelled him with scornful glance. "And as for you, I'd have been a damn sight better leaving you with the choir!" adding, sardonically, "but if you sing like you play football God help the choir!"

Alas, Mr. Henry never again considered him for the choir and during Shepy's short stay at Rosemount he never quite made it to the football team.

A vagabond goes to war

"C'mon now. Dinna greet. There's naethin' to worry aboot..."

WHEN HIS father's call-up papers arrived, the consequences didn't sink in with Shepy right away. From the first day of war all men between 18 and 41 had been liable for conscription. The youngest registered were summoned first, single men before married men, then married men with kids.

Of the three fighting services, his father stated a preference for the RAF. This gave Shepy a great sense of pride. It never entered his head that bomber crews faced a 50% wipe out or that his dad might become a rigger, fitter or mechanic. Most of his pals' fathers were over conscription age. Smike's father had seen action in World War I and had harrowing tales to tell. But that seemed old hat now.

So too were films Hells Angels and The Dawn Patrol which had deeply affected him, not withstanding his father's claims that the early 30s version of the latter – starring Richard Barthelmess – was better than the Errol Flynn re-make. But then he would wouldn't he?

Air aces Albert Ball, Eddie Rickenbacker and the Red Baron himself, Manfred von Richthofen were history to Shepy who thrilled to read The Camels are coming, with Biggles peering through the sights of the

Vickers guns on the cowling of his Sopwith Camel somewhere over France. And plane spotting was his latest hobby.

His Aunt Alice's brothers, Dave and Sandy, enlisted in the KOSB at the start. Junior footballer Jim Rankine, who always had a few minutes to spare with the kids in the street, and Smike's older brother Jack had joined the Navy. Sonny Foster across the road and Wullie, the jovial assistant in the corner grocer shop, were rear gunners on Lancaster bombers – suicide squad folk said.

Now Shepy reckoned he had something to crow about. His dad was doing something in the war. But as the departure day loomed an awareness of what his father's call-up would mean to him slowly penetrated his thinking. Activities taken for granted would no longer be the same minus the instigator-in-chief.

Shiftwork as hospital porter didn't prevent his father being a stagehand at HM Theatre. On the evenings that duty called he would take his leave singing some goodbye song or other, often "*I'm only a strolling vagabond, So goodnight pretty maiden, goodnight ...*" for the benefit of Shepy's mother, but enjoyed by them all.

Family visits to the Regent, Playhouse or Palace cinemas, all within easy walking distance, were undertaken every few weeks. Despite professed democratic views, Shepy's dad always chose the film, after all he was paying. But he rarely picked a stumor.

And what of card and board games? Bagatelle, lexicon and crown and anchor played by the family with scores scrupulously kept on the back of an envelope. Shepy's mother would be played upon and was easy to hoodwink. How they would miss the organisation and control his father exercised.

There were more important things like the stories his father read to them. The Water Babies and Hans Anderson led Shepy to Coral Island, Martin Rattler, Treasure Island and Tom Sawyer, still leaving time for Wizard, Hotspur and Frank Richard's creations Magnet and Gem, in their final throes due to paper shortage.

And in the back garden some years earlier, a lesson was learned in respect for nature when his father put a stop to him stunning bees with a Snappy Jack toy pistol before imprisoning them in a jar.

"Dae ye ken it tak's hunners o' bees to mak' honey for jist ae slice o' toast?" he censured. Henry Williamson on bees became required reading, then Salar the Salmon, Tarka the Otter and Jack London's White Fang and Call of the Wild.

Poems in vogue lampooning Hitler, Goering and Goebbels were hardly literary, and poetry at school was pretty soppy.

As to sport, he required no persuasion and was all ears to his father's appraisal of the greats in football, cricket, boxing, golf, billiards and horse racing – the last mentioned, as yet outwith Shepy's scope.

Assiduously collected from cigarette packets and comics, his photos of Willie Mills, Don Bradman, Joe Louis, Henry Cotton, Joe Davis and Gordon Richards were supplemented by gems collected in his father's youth – Alan Morton, Patsy Hendren, Jack Dempsey, Bobby Jones and Steve Donoghue – claimed to be better of course.

Politics were more difficult. He gathered that Russia had created a new civilisation, run by the people, on behalf of the people, free of our class system. Russians knew what they were fighting for as Uncle Joe Stalin presided over a truly democratic society with a just distribution of wealth.

Ah well. Shepy's father certainly wished for a better world, but even he couldn't be right all of the time.

The fateful day arrived. He would leave as if going to work. There would be no tearful parting at the station. Embraces were exchanged all round with special kisses for Shepy's younger sisters before he tucked a finger under Shepy's chin.

"You'll be man o' the hoose now" he pronounced. "So I'm gaein' ye my pocket watch."

Still a kid in short trousers, it was a heady moment for Shepy. It was a major step towards adulthood to receive a watch. Tears welled up in his eyes.

"C'mon now. Dinna greet. There's naethin' to worry aboot," assured his father. "If Beethoven and Burns can turn to dust, fa are we to worry?"

With a final hug and kiss for Shepy's mother he moved to the door and paused to sing.

"Even bravest hearts do swell
In the moment of farewell ..."
"I'm bound for the hills and the valleys beyond,
so goodbye my beloveds, goodbye ..."

And then he was gone.

Three-in-a-bedlam!

"C'MON NOW, behave yoursels! Stop rummlin aboot!" Shepy's mother stood in the bedroom doorway confronting three lively lads prancing, cavorting and threshing about on the bed like Dervishes.

Helping with evacuees seemed a laudable venture. But three kids in a bed, whichever way you looked at it, spelt bedlam as they tumbled and tossed about, bobbing up and down in one long, extended romp.

Older and bigger than Shepy, swarthy Roger Hernandez from Gibraltar was more a refugee than an evacuee. The son of Ellon farmer John Buchan (Big B) and nicknamed Smalbie (Small B) was slightly younger than Shepy.

Along with 10,500 other Gibraltarians, the Hernandez family arrived in this country after compulsory evacuation, to be introduced to identity cards, ration books and clothing coupons.

With Hitler offering up Gibraltar, parts of Algeria and Morocco, there were fears Franco would take Spain to war on the side of the Axis countries who helped him to power. It was not yet evident he would disappoint the Fuhrer and stay neutral.

Unfortunately the family were unable to find a place to take them all. Shepy's aunt Alice, in the same tenement, housed the middle-aged couple while Roger and his sister were billeted elsewhere.

That summer, so as the Hernandez family could be united for a spell, Shepy's mother gave Roger digs during school holidays, while a neighbour took on his engaging young student sister. Coinciding with this development, Shepy's grandmother in the ground floor was accommodating old friend Meg Buchan, her staff nurse daughter and Smalbie, reciprocating holidays spent at Little Arnage farm. Mother and daughter were welcome to her room bed-settee, but Smalbie would have to squeeze in with Shepy and Roger. The two young visitors lay one way with Shepy between them, head at bottom of the bed – between their feet! This invited the inevitable clowning, capering clamour and Shepy's mother's increasing annoyance.

"Jist fit's gaen on in here?" she railed. "Ye're waur nor bairns!"

A late child, Roger had been spoilt and indulged, and was hyperactive to boot. Indoors, his behaviour shocked even Shepy. Humble furniture and furnishings had scant regard from Roger.

Outdoors brought no improvement. Shepy had learned the hard way to respect neighbouring gardens. Roger had no such inhibitions.

Discovering Belisha Beacons revealed in Roger symptoms of anarchy.

At the last minute he would leap into the roadway in the path of traffic, daring them to run him down. Dialling numbers in telephone kiosks, he considered it hilarious hanging up when anyone answered.

What devastated Shepy, however, was the destruction of his cherished pre-war hollow-cast lead toy soldiers, no longer available in shops since production ceased for the duration.

Some had lost a little paint, but Shepy was aghast to find Dragoon Guards, turbanned Indian troopers and British Empire riflemen decapitated – mowed down by pencils propelled by the spring mechanism of a toy cannon. Minus limbs, lances and rifles, heads held on by matchsticks, his grenadiers, fusiliers and hussars would never be the same again.

"Michty me! Dinna rile me ony mair! Hud yer weesht an' get beddit doon." Shepy's mother sounded exasperated at the uproar as the knock-about continued apace.

Smalbie was more ill-tricked than destructive. Standing on a horse-drawn cart backed into Strachan's Gilcomston Mills, known as Coffee John's, a carter unloaded.

Creeping up to the horse, Smalbie jerked the reins and cried "Gee-up!" The unfortunate carter was thrown off his feet into the back of the cart. Shepy was well ahead as they fled up Jack's Brae round into Northfield.

Flush toilets were a novelty to Smalbie. Crossing from one stairhead lavatory to the other, continuously pulling the chain as each cistern refilled, he had to be prised away from his new-found pleasure.

At the cinema they were an embarrassment. Shepy didn't dare take them beyond the Cinema House or Belmont where the front bench seats didn't tip up noisily with their frequent trips to the toilet.

Both guests had voracious appetites and Shepy's mother was hard pressed making jam and syrup go round. Potatoes, dried eggs, dried milk and bread bridged the gap as Shepy and his sisters foraged along with their boarders. But for the moment rationing was not the problem.

"God be here! I winna tell ye again! I'm jist scunnered wi' the lot o' ye!" Shepy's mother had suffered about enough.

Suddenly there was an almighty crash. The bed finally gave up and collapsed under the combined boisterous bouncing bodyweight of the trio.

Things became somewhat quieter as the culprits spent the remainder of the night at floor level.

"I'm jist scunnered wi' the lot o' ye!"

Shepy remembered life in bed before his riotous bedmates materialised. But for the time being there was a war and he'd have to just grin and bear it.

The lodger and the chip cheat

"Jings whizz! At's a gey pucklie mair chips gin usual..."

"FAR HIV ye been?" his mother quizzed him. "Yer sister's awa' for Mr. Morrison's fish supper.

For Shepy to be late home from school was not unusual. It could be one of a number of things: playing in the street, visiting the library or kept in after school for some misdemeanour or other. But he'd never before slipped up on his regular chore.

Shepy's father was in the RAF and, for the family at home, existing on 38 shillings a week serviceman's pay was no mean feat. With young children to bring up it was difficult for his mother to work, so when a neighbour knew of a gentleman looking for digs Shepy's mother and father agreed she should go ahead and take in a lodger.

A Peterhead man, Bill Morrison served with HM Coastguard and had been posted to the station at Nigg. Bed and breakfast and evening meal was the arrangement. Except, that is, for his Friday night special treat when he paid out of his pocket for the fish and chips he loved.

Without fail Shepy received a threepenny tip for his labour but there was another incentive – a sneaky and ill-mannered one. Unravelling one end of the newspaper wrapping, he habitually helped himself to chips in the time it took to get home from the chip shop in Short Loanings, carefully tucking the folds in the paper back into place. Mr. Morrison never seemed to notice.

The new tenant impressed Shepy a great deal. A handy cricketer, he was soon fixed up with a club and played in the local grades. Watching him at the Links and Duthie Park, Shepy and his pals thought he bowled so fast they dubbed him the demon bowler.

He was also very generous. But when he invited Shepy's mother for an evening out, just to give her a treat in the midst of all the dreary austerity, she wouldn't go. She knew how people talked and she knew her place. So instead, he totted up his sweet coupons and gave her boxes of chocolates.

For a spell he actually shared a bed with Shepy. One day without warning, a collapsible bed chair, complete with three brown corduroy cushions and wire mattress, was delivered from the Equitable in St Nicholas Street. Shepy felt humiliated when the new resident announced he was fed up being kicked all over, had bruises to prove it, and was now going solo.

In the house he was very helpful, offering to do the dishes, and making himself generally useful. In the evenings there was nothing he liked more than sitting by the fireside reading or listening to the wireless, the £1 licence for which he insisted paying, grateful for a bit of home life, shared with a real family in his new-found home from home. Yet, he had a guilt complex about being in a reserved occupation while other men his age were being called-up. Some newspapers kept calling for an end to so-called deferment dodgers and there was a resurgence of white feathers. Many men were indeed involved in vital war work, and those exempted on medical grounds were issued with badges, but for the rest, well ... if the cap fitted?

And this inner conflict gave vent to their paying guest's one apparent weakness. Not infrequently he would come home and flop into his bed chair in an inebriated state, heaving maudlin sighs that he was tired of getting dirty looks and calling for heaven to witness that he'd tried to enlist, but they kept turning him down because of his job. "War hath no fury like a non-combatant," he would quote bitterly.

He also had a peroxide blonde girl friend and took her back to the house. There was a desperate shortage of cosmetics, yet Shepy was fascinated by the heavily applied rouge and lip stick make-up which made her look like one of his sister's big dolls, but merely excited disapprobation in his mother.

"Nae need to clart a bonny face like yon," she said, damning her with faint praise.

Shepy was further bewitched, by her luscious tan-painted legs – a consequence of the scarcity of silk stockings, with nylons yet to come. So intrigued was he by her showy legs he contrived in the course of his floor games to position himself under the table where, thanks to her short utility skirt, he could satisfy his curiosity about how far up the colouring went.

The table was set and Mr. Morrison sat in his usual place scanning the Evening Express, still only one penny but reduced to four pages because of the news print shortage.

He was reading aloud about the local tribunal appearance of a conscientious objector who admitted he'd just been released from prison after serving 30 days for beating up his grandmother, and they were all having a laugh about it when Shepy's sister came in with his fish supper.

Quickly removing the wrapping, Shepy's mother piled the contents on to her boarder's plate. Lowering the newspaper he was reading Mr. Morrison's eyes immediately widened at the heaped dish before him.

"Jings whizz! At's a gey pucklie mair chips gin usual," he enthused.

Shepy blushed a bright scarlet. His pilfering game had been exposed and he felt a deep sense of shame at being found out.

"Ye little divil. Ye've been pinchin' Mr. Morrison's chips!" Shepy's mother gave him a dunt. "Ye mak' me black-affrontit."

Mr. Morrison threw back his head, smote his thighs and laughed heartily, teasing Shepy that he'd get his sister to go next time. Still chuckling away he thrust a threepenny-bit into Shepy's hand.

"Here ye are loon. Awa' roon and get yer ration. I widna want to dae ye oot o' yer chips the nicht noo, wid I?"

Shepy faces the rap

"THERE is no possible excuse whatsoever for such unworthy behaviour."

Tawse in hand, the towering, awesome figure stepped round the desk and faced the three boys. Shepy and his classmates were in at the deep end. They just hadn't considered the consequences of their escapade and now faced the moment of truth.

It had been a disastrous month for Shepy. Apparently unable to keep out of trouble, he had fallen foul of several teachers.

His early morning paper round up Rosemount for Duncan's at the top of Watson Street caused him to dose off during the geography lesson. Shepy could just about cope with capital cities, longest rivers and highest mountains.

But in her voluminous skirt and tent-like top and brandishing a large gold wristlet watch on a loose gold bracelet which she kept flipping to bring the watch right side-up, rotund geography mistress Miss Dalgliesh, known as "Dally", would drone on interminably about isotherms and isobars, cumulus and nimbus, table-land and tundra.

Unable to answer or indeed repeat her question, he was sent from the room to languish outside the door for his bad manners, prey to his headteacher or head master on the prowl.

Shepy was also no favourite of Miss Adams, a fiery, florid-faced, French-speaking Ma Broon with a temper which made him nervous. His oral French and class rating suffered as a result, although his written work was fair to average. In the latest paper, for the report cards, he exceeded all expectations.

"Plookie", as thc peppery French mistress was dubbed, construing his vocal howlers deliberate and disruptive, grudged his ranking above those she favoured and let him know volubly.

Now, he and his schoolmates received a dressing down from none other than the formidable Central School "heedie" Jock Robertson himself, a man not given to dealing with trivialities. Well schooled by older pupils of Jock's prowess, Shepy eyed the leather strap folded in the headmaster's hand as he addressed them.

"You so-called sportsmen have set a very low example for this school."

Of course, Shepy was not attending the "real" Central School on the corner of Belmont Street and Schoolhill. That premises had been requisitioned as a hospital, just as in World War I. Central pupils now shared the Grammar School. And its proximity to Shepy's home address got him in further trouble. School gates were shut when school was in and during playtime intervals. Skinny enough to wriggle through the space at a bent railing opposite Northfield, Shepy regularly slipped home for refreshments.

Some visits proved auspicious enough, as when he burst in on the arrival into the world of his second sister, or met up with his father, home on leave with a Mintlaw airman friend who was later to die in action.

Such absences, however, were frowned upon. Spotted or caught getting back after the bell merited the belt, lines, extra homework or detention after school.

Earlier that week in the "huts", Nissen prefabs furnished with single desks and unsuitable wicker chairs, set up in the grounds to accommodate extra classes, Shepy just made it, but became immediately, embroiled in a frantic "pass the chair" tussle to avoid being lumbered with the unwelcome wobbly one.

"I'm not disturbing you, am I?" suave, dapper maths master Freddy Falconer asked sarcastically as he strode in on the fracas. He then went into his Dave Willis routine: a vigorous tugging at his jacket and exaggerated panting, "Hold me back! Hold me back!" At the end of his charade he calmly proceeded to belt each of the boys involved.

When it came to being strapped by science master Mr. Menzies, however, it hurt the school's most gentlemanly staff member as much as it hurt Shepy. Some thing in Shepy's nature didn't hold with taking advantage of kindly or "soft" teachers reluctant to use the tawse.

But caught red-handed along with "Ping" Ingram flicking ink-pellets at Kenny Thomson who had doused them with a Bunsen burner connected to the water tap in the science room, poor Mr. Menzies had really no alternative but to administer the belt.

In thc year before the war, in front of a crowd exceeding 90,000, Second Division East Fife had won the Scottish Cup, accounting for Aberdeen along the way. Several members of that cup-winning team were in the side to meet the Dons in a war-time North Eastern League match at Pittodrie. And seeing them was a fancy that grew to a longing which became a dire necessity by Saturday.

There was certainly no mistaking the reason for Shepy and his classmates appearance before the rancorous headmaster. Wartime priorities required Grammar and Central pupils to attend half-days including Saturdays. School on a Saturday morning seemed punishment enough. But on an afternoon it became a form of torture. Central were on afternoons that month so Shepy & Co. had played truant.

But had it all been worth it? They were finding out.

"There are people making sacrifices and suffering discomforts far greater than attending school on a Saturday afternoon," sneered the headmaster contemptuously in his final admonition before delivering six strokes to each boy, three on either hand.

Leaving the headmaster's room to return to his class, Shepy thought of his eager anticipation to see the match, then of his apprehension of punishment at Jock Robertson's hands. In the event both proved anti-climaxes. The match was a damp squib and the "scudding" hadn't hurt that much. The "heedie" had made him feel unsportsmanlike so perhaps it was fitting that he derived no pleasure from the whole affair.

Nothing but the best

IT WAS the grocer on Leadside corner, Peter Yule, who fired him up, planting the seed as it were. Once it took root, however, there was no diverting Shepy.

The elder of his two sisters had pricked his conscience initially. The problem was what to give their mother for her birthday, virtually a first time for Shepy, more accustomed to dwelling on the receiving end at birthdays.

But they couldn't decide on a gift. Whatever they bought her she would say: "Ye shouldna've spint a' that on me", then, in her selfless way, give it to someone, share it out or alter it to fit a family member.

"Why divn't ye tak' her oot fer a meal," suggested the shop keeper. "An' I dinna mean the placey next door," he added, alluding to the simply-furnished British Restaurant offering a wholesome three-course lunch of beef, two veg., treacle pud and cup of tea for a shilling.

Shepy warmed to the dapper, dark-haired grocer who was well patronised by the kids.

"Gi'er a treat. Tak' her tae the Caley, no less," he urged Shepy. "At's fit ti dae. Jist book in an' tell the manager I sent ye."

Raising money was the hard bit. Every penny they could lay their hands on was saved, from coppers earned running errands to their own pocket money.

Pooling their resources in this way amassed 10 shillings. Lodger Bill Morrison added a half crown sighing, with tongue in cheek, "Weel, sine she winna gang oot wi' me."

Noted for its excellent cuisine, the Caledonian Hotel was one of Aberdeen's most ornate eating places. It could well have been the Ritz or Savoy to Shepy, climbing the broad steps to be confronted by a big doorman.

"I want to see the manager," said Shepy, his voice wavering. The doorman was either impressed by his earnestness or in a good mood for he bade Shepy follow him through the sumptuous foyer to the manager's office.

Shepy had never been in a hotel before. With burnished brass, mirrored walls and luxurious banqueting suites, everything glowed and shimmered.

"A young gent to see you Mr. Mercer," winked the doorman at the hotel boss seated at his desk, and withdrew.

“What can I do for you young man?” queried the genial manager. Shepy explained as best he could about his mother’s birthday, his sisters and that he had 12s.6d. Oh yes! And that Peter Yule had sent him.

“Is that so,” said the manager. “Hmm. We’ll have to see what we can do.” Opening a ledger on his desk he made a note and looked up. “I think we can fit you in.”

The day arrived. The circle Rosemount tram stopped right opposite the hotel. They walked inside to a throbbing hub of excitement as a crowd of fashionable folk awaited admittance. Shepy gulped, went fearfully up to the red-coated attendant and blurted out details of the reservation.

Like magic they were swept through to be met by the head waiter. “Right this way,” he smiled, leading them across the room past crisply set tables, each with a perfect pink rose in small white vase, to a table by the window overlooking the terrace gardens.

The place began to fill up. A dressy, flamboyant couple occupied the adjoining table. Both smoked, had been drinking and were rather mouthy.

...he bade Shepy follow him through the sumptuous foyer...

Dinner began. Silver sparkled and crystal glistened. First course on the menu, soupe du jour, turned out to be leek and potato. Their florid-faced neighbour leaned towards them.

"At's nae soup da joor ye ken," he enlightened them. Bemused, Shepy's mother raised her eye brows. "Isn't it?" she asked meekly.

"Naw," he confided knowingly out of the side of his mouth. "I hid soup da joor at a weddin' aince, an' it wis chicken!"

The dinner continued. Service was constant, attentive and each course seemed better than the one before. As they sat there in a glow of happiness the head waiter suddenly appeared.

Opening a bottle of "something" with a subdued "pop" he filled the glasses. Shepy's mother was presented with a lovely little birthday cake, a small posy of flowers and an inscribed card. There was a roll of drums and the resident trio played "Happy birthday to you."

The boorish gent accosted the waiter standing by. "Hey Charly, did I tell ye aboot mi new car?"

"No," answered the waiter, "and I certainly appreciate it."

When the bill arrived it was for 12s.6d., exactly what Shepy told Mr. Mercer he could afford. It was clear, even to Shepy, that this amount couldn't possibly begin to cover the cost.

He looked up open-mouthed at the waiter who smiled and said, "All the staff hope you enjoyed the meal."

On shelves somewhere in the Caledonian Hotel there will no doubt be records of famous guests and notable events. One occasion is not included – when kind, warm-hearted, good natured people provided happiness for an ordinary family's big day out.

If the hotel was a bit tatty during the war – plaster flaking, paint-work fading, carpeting had seen better days – then Shepy didn't notice. It was a day he'd never forget.

He had quite a story for Peter Yule next time in his shop, telling him that his connection had worked wonders.

Peter chuckled. "I'm richt gled for ye, but I've niver met the man. I widna ken 'im fae Adam."

Shepy's face-saver

The fiercely driven ball caught him full in the face

"WHEEP!" The referee's whistle signalled kick-off. Auchnagatt's centre-forward "Shooders" Tamson, so-called due to his massive breadth, sprang forward. Disdaining a short pass to either inside forward, he uttered a loud whoop as if exhorting a cavalry charge and blasted the ball straight ahead.

Standing directly opposite on the centre circle, eyes screwed up against the sun, Shepy was completely unprepared for such unorthodoxy. The fiercely driven ball caught him full on the face, lifted him off his feet and threw him flat on his back. Semi-conscious, he was carried to the touchline where efforts were made to revive him.

Recent weeks on the 80-acre smallholding of his granny's freens, John (known as Bigbie) and Meg Buchan, had dispelled Shepy's romantic notion of life on the farm. Early mornings, long back-breaking drudgery in the field and all-pervading smells soon apprised him of the reality.

And now, after weeks coling hay, hoeing neep dreels, stooking and stacking corn, cleaning out barn and byre, sty and stable, often made aware of his lack of expertise, what may just have been the culminating, redeeming event in a lengthy "work his keep" holiday at Little Arnage appeared to have bitten the dust – literally!

Shapely young Betty Buchan, her greenhorn brother Ian (dubbed Smalbie) and, most important of all, fee't loon Airchie Gavin would not now see his performance. Actually, although the course of events now indicated otherwise, Shepy was lucky to be in the side. Team captain Airchie, small and wiry himself, saw him as a shargart toonser amang strappin' country chiels.

In the amusement arcade of a travelling fun fair on Udny Green, a "beat the goalie" booth, with all comers invited to try and score, gave Shepy an opportunity to perform his spot-kick trick. After the fashion of Don's war-time goal-scoring guest-star Ernie Waldron, he made to shoot with his left foot, quickly stepped forward on same foot and side-footed the ball home with his right, deceiving the keeper, and sufficiently impressing Airchie to recruit him as centre forward.

Wind and rain lashed his face as he recovered. Where was he? He could remember Burnett's red New Deer bus in Mealmarket Street and getting off at Turnerhall Smiddy; fishing the Ythan and Ebrie burn and picking wild rasps in Plodhill wood; fantasising Wells Fargo on horse-drawn, two-wheel box cairt trips to Ellon mart and dressing up for the fairmers' dance at Drumwhindle school. Now he faced the elements?

He opened his eyes cautiously. Betty was briskly fanning him with a large towel while Meg zealously squeezed a sponge over his stinging face. Wind and rain indeed. Now coming round he could hear their shouts.

"Dis it nae coont fan they kick oor Smalbie or maun they ca 'im ower a'thigither?" shrieked Meg.

"Foo lang dae ye hae tae be a half-back afore they mak' ye a full-back?" Betty teased Airchie.

Substitutes hadn't been invented and, on his feet now, Shepy was waved back on to the pitch. Desperate to get in touch with the play he ran about a great deal but to little avail. Passing was virtually non-existent as the ball was thumped enthusiastically from end to end in a rollicking game of aerial football.

There was no mistaking the opposition's danger man. At regular intervals bodies were carted to the touchline, having collided with, been mistaken for the ball by, or like Shepy, got in the way of a ferocious drive from the ubiquitous Shooders Tamson.

The battle raged on into the second half and was drawing to a close with neither side apparently capable of scoring. Shepy, who had rarely been in the game, watched depressed as the ball was booted for the umpteenth time high and wide out of the park.

In the distance wee kids fastened on it, beginning an impromptu game of their own. Players stood around in groups talking and enjoying the sun.

At long last the ball came sailing over the heads of the crowd on the touchline to be caught involuntarily by Smalbie reclining against a goalpost. Shaping to lob it back for the throw-in he was stopped in his tracks by a shrill blast from the referee who pointed dramatically to the spot.

Pandemonium broke loose and a heated argument ensued as the referee was surrounded by protesting players.

"Ye canna mean it ref!" howled Airchie. "Ye're haiverin'". But the whistler was adamant. Unobserved by the unwitting Smalbie a long throw actually had been taken by a player obscured by spectators on the line. Airchie, livid with rage, had more to say on the matter and collared the badgered official.

"Hey ref! Fut wid ye dae gin I ca'd ye a gypit neep-heided gollach?"

"I'd hae tae order ye aff," came the blunt reply.

"Weel, fut wid ye dae gin I jist thocht it?" Airchie countered doggedly."The referee considered for a moment. "Gin ye only thocht it, I couldna send ye aff," he concluded.

"Weel, I think ye're a gypit neep-heided gollach!" avowed Airchie.

The official reddened but, with the game in its final minute, decided he could do without an ordering off, concentrating all his efforts in getting the penalty taken. But Airchie persisted, and confronted his arbiter.

"Can I be excused aff the pitch for a minute?"

"Fut for?" fumed the angry referee.

"I wid like to go and feed yer guide dog."

"Queel doon. I'll hae nae mair yaummerin'," he warned, placing the ball on the spot as Shooders Tamson sauntered up.

This was it. Shepy could have wept. Shooder's incredible kicking power was said to have burst goal-nets, winded goalkeepers and actually broken a crossbar. Everyone went up for the penalty while Shepy stood alone and downcast just inside his own half.

Shuffling forward the Auchnagatt stalwart smote the ball with tremendous force. Eyes closed, the nervous goalkeeper threw up his arms to shield his face as the thunderous shot crashed against the bar with such impact that the ball rebounded in a great soaring arc all the way to the centre circle.

Shepy watched incredulous as the ball bounced before him. Trapping it, at second attempt in his excitement, he sped off unhindered. Veering away from the advancing keeper, he steered the ball into the vacant goal. There was no time to centre the ball.

The bruising on Shepy's face was visible for several days. The euphoria was evident for somewhat longer.

Crisp injustice

AT the top of the Brae, on Leadside corner, Shepy stood solemnly among a group of youngsters patiently awaiting the homecoming of Stewart Rae. Known as Stew, he lived in humble circumstances a few doors down the Brae, just beyond Strachan's Mills and directly opposite Shepy's granny's cooked food shop.

Stew's mother had died in childbirth and his unemployed father had scarpered to the States, leaving a spinster Aunt Jean to bring him up single-handed. A hard-working, selfless little woman who slaved away daily at Harrott's glove and hosiery factory on Rose Street, she was about the only person to call him by his proper Christian name.

Both Stew and his aunt regularly frequented the handy little food shop as Jean, working full-time, was rushed at the dinner hour to cook for her growing nephew. Almost daily she or Stew would collect portions of Scotch broth, skirlie, stovies, tripe and onions or freshly made potted head, taken away in their own trays, bowls, jugs or even jam-jars. Her considerable tick was paid up on Saturdays when she received her pay.

Stew and Shepy enjoyed frequent contact through school, shop and paper-round duties. Their fondness for each other was mutual. A big, shy, gentle lad, slightly older than Shepy, Stew was in the same class at school as he was repeating a year. He had a wretched speech defect and had to tolerate some banter from his schoolmates when he stammered and stuttered nervously. No malice may have been intended, but he was self-conscious about his impediment and more so when his nickname all too often degenerated from Stew Rae to "Stumer" or "Stuttery".

Many of the boys had nicknames, some affectionate, some cruel, and they didn't come any crueller than ascribed to Stew. Shepy knew all about nicknames, but he drew the line with a few others at an appellation which, scarcely subtle, was a pitiless mockery of Stew's disability.

There was no doubt whatsoever that people in the Place thought themselves superior to those on the somewhat dingy Brae. Also evident was a tendency to talk down to Stew as though he needed to have things explained very simply. But Stew knew far more words than most of them. Articulating them was something else, but he remained brave and dauntless in his quest for respect and acceptance.

Ready, willing and able, he loved football and could run fast which helped his self-esteem. But he would get overexcited, and suddenly start uttering loud, shrill, ear-splitting shrieks, trying to make himself understood. Then followed the sniggers, the ridicule, the humiliation and misery etched on his stricken, unsmiling face.

Stew needed no looking after. He could take care of himself, but it would never have occurred to the long-suffering youth to thump any of those kids who had little idea of how much they hurt him.

That's why, when he was asked by some of the lads to store two large cardboard boxes in his basement cellar on the Brae, with no questions asked, so anxious was he to please and ingratiate himself with his pals that he readily agreed, without thinking of any possible consequences.

"Dinna tell onybody onything," they urged. "Say naething to naebody." Stew smiled, thinking wistfully that speech is silver, but silence is golden.

The following day the police came and went – with Stew. In the course of their enquiries they had soon been led to the ne'er-do-well Brae, and it didn't require great sleuthing to trace the whereabouts of the boxes. Only Stew fetched coal and firewood from the cellar, so his Aunt Jean would have suspected nothing.

"Fit hiv ye dane Stewart?" she sobbed as they led him out. "I dae my best for ye." Stew hung his head in undeserved shame as he was taken to Lodge Walk to be detained overnight in a cell.

Now filled with trepidation at what Stew might reveal to the police, the gang sat tight and waited with baited breath until the court case came up.

The plan had formed when a member of the gang maintained adamantly that the tenant on the Place had himself pinched the boxes – containing much sought after potato crisps – from his employers, stowed them in his backyard cellar and so was hardly likely to report the matter to the police. A very wrong assumption as it turned out. The tenant had bought them wholesale.

When the case came up Stew was charged in the city's juvenile court with breaking and entering, theft while acting with others unknown and harbouring stolen goods. The threat of Oakbank was a well-known warning to delinquent youths and kept many in check. The ever constant Stew said nothing to incriminate any of his pals and was sent to the approved school for boys for three months.

But every cloud has a silver lining. At Oakbank, Stew's speech problem was diagnosed by a top specialist to be caused by enlarged tonsils. After treatment his speech improved, with an expectation that he should speak quite normally in a matter of months.

At last, after six weeks in custody, model first offender Stew was granted early release. With his devoted aunt, he got off the Rosemount tram on the Viaduct at the foot of Leadside. When they appeared around the corner of the Brae a cheer immediately went up. Stew looked much older, taller and very healthy.

"Fit like Stew?" Foo ye deein'?" they cried. "Three cheers for good old Stew!" The partially conscience-stricken kids considered him a local hero the way he had taken the rap for them all.

Stew's Aunt Jean was in tears at their welcome and he wasn't very far behind, his speech faltering as he continually hugged her.

"Gee it's g-gran' to be hame again. Thanks tae ye all for the w-welcome. I r-really appreciate ye all t-turning oot like this." They all blinked in surprise and disbelief. No sign of bitterness or resentment.

With his devoted aunt, he got off the Rosemount tram on the Viaduct at the foot of Leadside.

Scarcely a trace of his stutter.

"Fit like wis the grub Stewart?" asked Shepy without really thinking.

"P-pretty awful," answered Stew, "c-caul doughballs and p-porridge a' the time." He grinned. "It wis jist the thocht o' g-getting back to Grunny Sutherland's p-potted heid that kept me gyaun".

Stew was unlikely to be belittled in future. Not after what he had done to keep them in the clear. And his speech difficulty, with the correct treatment, would no longer be risible.

Things wouldn't change overnight, but a start had been made, and the rest would soon follow the leaders. It was ever thus. Stew, as the trite old saying goes, had paid his debt to society. In doing so the strange ways of fate had seen fit to diagnose and correct his affliction. He hadn't quite stumbled over his last syllable, but he still knew more words than most.

Now he could give voice to them.

A wee slip tae the loo

The little girl simply folded up like a penknife

I WANT to go to the big ane," whined Shepy's little sister. "I want to go on the big seat."

To say that Shepy was fed up was a gross understatement. The wee lass, a wartime baby spoiled by a doting father when home on leave and accustomed to getting her own way, probably thought she was old enough.

Yet he had no intention of taking her downstairs to the lavatory on the landing. Stubbornly, he stuck her on the chamber pot kept under the sink for that purpose and told her to get on with it.

So doing, he returned to the green baize-covered table to resume the game he was endeavouring to play with his toddler cousin Gordon who was even younger than his lively little sister.Of course, there was more to his low spirits than the over-ambitious demands of his precocious sister. It had to be said, however, that they were entirely self-inflicted.

At the top of Northfield, just across the way from the "Maggie a'thing" corner shop run by spinster sisters Maggie and Katie Willox, was a neat stone wall some 12 by six feet, near perfect for a make-believe goal, with a coping for a crossbar. And if Shepy had been a trifle less vainglorious about his left foot he need never have come to grief in the way that he did.

Nonchalantly side-footing a tennis ball against the wall from all angles he would occasionally drive the ball back fiercely, having a "shot at goal" as it were. Accomplishing a left foot shot, kids would brag, "see, 'at wis wi' mi left fit!" Shepy didn't hesitate when the ball broke to his left.

Well, you've guessed. He didn't connect properly and the ball shattered a panel in the window of the adjacent house. Living nearby, there was no escape.

"Trust you, fin it's new fowk jist intae that hoose as weel," fumed his mother. "It's a good job yer faither's nae here, ye muckle gype 'at ye are."

But she was staggered by the note sent charging for the damage. Discussed solemnly, at great length, in his granny's flat, where his mother and aunties congregated for their regular fly-cup, his uncle Dave, a tile-fixer with Middler's specialising in stepped tiled fireplaces which, despite the war, were all the rage replacing the old iron grates in the homes of those who could afford it, who "just happened" to be in the vicinity in time for a fly-cup, was moved to comment.

"Phew! Michty me, at's a bit steep I wid say. Gi'es a hud o't. I'll hae a wordie aboot it."

That afternoon the womenfolk went to see wedding gifts of a neighbour's daughter. After his misdeed, Shepy had no option but to stay in looking after his little sister and wee Gordon.

The arrangement mortified Shepy. The Dons were playing away so he'd intended seeing a film of a new American comic team Abbott and Costello at the Playhouse with his pals. Now he was stuck with two kids at too tender an age for his liking.

Determined, as always, to salvage what he could from the fate which had befallen him, Shepy left his sister to her dolls and sweet ration and decided to set up the table cricket created by his dad, recruiting willing wee Gordon for the bowling.

This was achieved by dropping a ball bearing down a peashooter held at an angle on one side of the table so it rolled swiftly towards the "wicket" at the opposite side.

This "batsman" was a small gear wheel fixed to a steel rod suspended between Meccano set uprights on flanged plates, raised then released by means of a cord, hopefully to make contact with the ball now speeding towards the miniature metal wicket.

This gallows-like, Heath Robinson contraption worked well. The wheel sent the ball in all directions: over the run-numbered lines on the baize, or into the hands of cardboard fielders, made by his uncle George and glued to a circular plywood base carved out to "catch" the ball.

In this manner Shepy re-lived Test action, his MCC heroes Len Hutton and Denis Compton trading cover drives with Australians Don Bradman and Lindsay Hassett. No bowlers?

Wee nipper Gordon, keen as mustard, was just too young to bowl accurately. Shepy grew frustrated releasing the wheel only for it to swing in space as the ball rolled wide. Hitting the ball off the table was a six, but the ball finished on the floor more often as the tiny fellow fumbled slotting it down the peashooter.

To make matters worse his indefatigable little sister got on his nerves with her constant protestations to go to the big lavvy.

Meanwhile, in the world outside, uncle Dave called on the neighbours with the broken window. They had no inkling he was a relative of Shepy.

"I see ye've a broken windae," he addressed the man of the house. "I'm in the trade and could fix it fer ye fer fifteen shillins."

"Awa' ye go. Fit div ye tak' me for," the man glowered. "That job's nae worth a ha' penny mair nor siven and sixpence."

"A'richt, at's fair enough. Here's yer siven and six," agreed Dave. "I'm the loon fa broke yer windae's uncle, and here's the note you sent charging a pound. Ye ken fit ye can dae wi't."

Popping in with the news for Shepy to relate to his mother when she returned, uncle Dave had just left when Shepy's single-minded sister started a fresh campaign in her resolve to use the grown-up's toilet.

"I want to go to the big ane this time," she wailed. "I want to go on the big seat."

Either his uncle's sharp-witted solution to the window-cost crisis relieved his gloom, or his kid sister finally wore him down. Whatever it was he at last relented. Marching the wee madam downstairs to the WC, he planted her on the wooden seat and let her go.

The result was quite remarkable. The little girl simply folded up like a penknife, with only her head and feet visible as she sank screaming into the bowl.

Shepy got a right telling-off later, but his little sister never again asked him to take her to the "big ane".

The bird and the pussy-cat

GRIM-FACED, Shepy climbed over the wooden palings at the foot of the drying green and descended into the depths of the Mackie Place hollow, where the Denburn flowed tirelessly through to the sea. Somewhere down there he hoped to find her alive, but amongst the profusion of trees, thickets and dense foliage his chances looked remote.

Making his way alongside the burn, he became aware suddenly of something moving and wriggling about in the water. Shallow at that point he could see it was a small sack which kept bobbing up and down. Curious, he approached warily, picked up a broken branch and gingerly poked the squirming bundle.

He jumped back startled as the sack writhed about with increased intensity, and was nervous about opening it up lest he unloosed a ferret, stoat, rat or anything that might bite…

It was Saturday morning. Shepy was raking up leaves thick on the drying green, hemmed in on either side by neighbouring back gardens on the Place and the Avenue, and at the foot, by fencing protecting the "out of bounds" Mackie Place coppice from where most of the leaves had blown. He would have been happy enough to let them ultimately blow away, but he had to earn his pocket money somehow.

Never loath to remind anyone within range that he had once worked for a jobbing gardener, albeit a neighbour, for the duration of his school holidays one year – so making matters horticultural mere child's play – his smug reverie was interrupted suddenly by a nervous young female blackbird hopping anxiously just inches ahead of his rake.

"Whoops!" cried Shepy trying to avoid her. The bird was dishevelled and disorientated, hobbling and stumbling as she spread her wings, hovering scarcely a foot off the ground. It was obvious she couldn't launch herself into the air, crippled perhaps as a result of falling from the nest.

There were still a few breadcrumbs on the wash-house roof, scattered there earlier by his mother. Well away from cats perhaps, but also well out of reach of his new found forlorn friend.

"Hey ma! We've got a wee blackie," he yelled as he dashed through the porch and up the back stairs, to return moments later with a chipped enamel bowl and some bread which he quickly broke into pieces.

Eager and excited the bird, which Shepy instantly dubbed

"Whoopsie", jumped up to snatch the bread from his fingers, gobbling it down ravenously. He left the bird eating the remainder of the bread while he went to fill the bowl with water from the wash-house tap.

Emerging with the bowl cupped in his hands, he was aghast to see the sleek form of a big gingery-brown cat slowly stalking the poor bird, fluttering desperately just ahead of her raptor, jumping as high as her unsteady legs would allow.

Low to the ground and ready to pounce, the cat was playing with its prey. A shiver ran down Shepy's spine. Was it a feral cat or even a wildcat? Perhaps it was one of Mrs Sanderson along the road's many cats. He didn't wait to ask.

"Shoo! Shoo!!" he gesticulated, pitching the dish of water over the cat, gratefully relieved to see it dart over the fence into the undergrowth.

Cats like hunting birds as much as they like to play cat and mouse, finding birds, however, more difficult to catch. But poor Whoopsie, who couldn't even get up to perch on a branch, was a sitting target, and right then Shepy's feeling for cats was equivocal.

Meanwhile the bird resumed her feeding, voraciously clearing the lot. Flapping her wings she then hopped into the bowl, enjoying a drink and a bath at the same time.

When eventually she jumped from the bowl, she toppled over and landed on her back, legs threshing the air, struggling to get back on her feet. With a little support from Shepy she regained her poise and began to preen her ragged plumage, putting a fresh dark sheen on her feathers. She then hopped to the foot of the green and ducked under the fence. Wings stretched, she plunged clumsily into the undergrowth, returning instinctively, or so Shepy wistfully thought, to her natural habitat. How wrong he was.

Next morning, as Shepy washed his face at the kitchen sink, he was amazed to see the bird there on the back green wiping her blunt brown beak on the grass, like a barber strops his razor, awaiting her breakfast.

"She's bin waitin' for ye," laughed his mother.

"Fit wye dae ye ken it's a she?" he asked.

"Weel, she's got a broon beak. It's the male fa's got a yellow ane."

Once more he gathered some bread and ran downstairs to do the needful, finding her quivering with recognition and anticipation when she saw him, before satisfying her almost unimaginable appetite.

And this routine was to continue for several days. The bird would arrive between 8 and 9 am for breakfast, have a bath, stay for lunch and in the early evening after supper would busy herself in the back green poking her beak in the ground foraging after worms and grubs. Then she adjourned for the night to Mackie Place thicket.

As the days passed she rallied a bit more, flexing her muscles and wings. Although she still stumbled and fell about, there seemed a gradual improvement as she got stronger each day.

Shepy had noted her getting up waist high in her endeavours to evade the cat. Perhaps she would yet fly. Meanwhile, she hopped about with a springy, chirpy erectness, full of confidence and expectation, beak ever open to be fed.

All through the night the rains came in a drenching downpour. In the morning, when she showed up, eyes blinking miserably, plumage wet and bedraggled, she looked really sorry for herself.

That day, because the family were visiting friends and wouldn't be back until mid-evening, Whoopsie was fed early and cheered up considerably. Shepy felt uneasy on departure, and more so when there was no sign of her on their return. But he comforted himself with the thought that in his absence she had pitched camp somewhere in Mackie Place shrubbery and that it was just a matter of time before she popped up again.

But it was not to be. The following day came and went and still there was no sign of her. The loss to him was almost unendurable, but by evening he was becoming resigned to the fact. Had she flown off at last? Had she become the victim of a predatory cat?

"It's nae eese mopin' ye ken," consoled his mother. "Ye canna keep a birdie like that in captivity." But he wouldn't rest until he knew.

As he climbed down into Mackie Place in search of Whoopsie, his hopes were not high and, downcast at the turn of events, he walked despondently alongside the burn, vainly peering in the bushes and shrubbery and then it was he came upon the sack floundering in the water, and began his suspicious probing.

Suddenly a plaintive 'miaow' emanated from within the bag. With a great sense of relief he hurriedly disentangled the knot to reveal a wee, wet, bewildered kitten, just a few inches long, the tiniest he had ever seen, with a sparkling black and silvery grey pelage and saucer-like green eyes. Tenderly he picked up the soaked, fluffy handful which, left to drown, now purred hopefully as he gently stroked it.

"Gosh," he gasped, spellbound by the sheer charm of the lovely little creature, becoming a devotee of the species there and then.

"How could onybody dae this?" And then he gulped as he

Shepy climbed over the wooden palings at the foot of the drying green and descended into the depths of the Mackie Place hollow

remembered the events that had led him to the burn in the first place.

Nature can be cruel indeed, relentlessly taking its course. Sadly, he had lost the hapless Whoopsie, but he now had a new responsibility, and his furry foundling was probably a better bet for a pet. His mum had a soft spot for animals so he confidently took his feline friend home for the customary saucer of milk.

"Hey ma! Fit dae ye think ma! Wi've got a wee kitten." He would soon learn that cats could be semi-wild, independent free spirits by nature. But with ears pricked up, nose wrinkled and tail twitching, his pocket-sized pal fixed him with an attentive stare and purred approvingly.

Counting the days

THE air-raid practice more or less put paid to the French lesson. When the alarm sounded, a mass exodus of the entire school commenced. In approximately three minutes no one was to be seen above ground in the west field, although many strange noises issued from the murky depths of the shelters as pupils and teachers tripped to and fro along the 8inch planks, not infrequently enquiring if they were in the correct section.

After the drill Miss Adams, irreverently called "Plookie" by the pupils, utilised the brief time remaining to display her modest collection of past and present French coins, passing them round the class and remarking on their unique design, historical significance and exceptional intrinsic value.

"Regardez le sou et deux sous," she gushed. "Percevoyez la similarité to our ha'penny and penny."

The bell rang just as the coins reached Shepy and deskmate Bill Milne. With unusual nonchalance the French mistress motioned them to retain the coins between them to examine at leisure at home.

More to Shepy's liking was word on the notice board that he was a prize-winner in the schools essay competition on wartime fire dangers and would receive ten bob in savings stamps. Not for the first time he'd been coached by his father, fortuitously on leave and well-versed in incendiary bombs, highly inflammable substances and stirrup pumps.

That evening Shepy again met up with Bill Milne at the North Kirk youth club. Having outgrown Skene Square and Skene Street play centres, he didn't grudge the long walk to the popular Queen Street club ministered by Revs. Lees and Symington. With walking sticks held the other way round, keenly fought duster hockey took place in the hall despite the intrusive massive columns supporting the roof. And the badminton, table tennis and indoor football under the amiable eye of St Clements and Arbroath pivot Gus McGillivray; all this plus tea and home baking available for a few coppers in the offering box.

Next day, on the way to headmaster Jock Robertson's room to collect his savings stamps, Shepy met up with Ginger McGregor, a chirpy older boy in the school football team. Ginger had lined up a job but required his leaving certificate to secure it. He knew he had passed from lists posted on the notice board and hoped Jock would release it to him in advance.

Arriving at the headmaster's door, Ginger knocked and waited. After a lengthy pause he knocked once more. Nothing happened. He knocked a third time. Still no response. He put his ear to the door. There was no sound. Hesitantly, Ginger turned the knob, eased open the door and peered in.

Jock glowered across his desk. "How dare you enter before being invited!" he barked. "Get out at once and knock!"

Ginger jumped back as if he'd been stung, closing the door in the same movement. Taking a deep breath he glanced at Shepy, exhaling a loud "phew!" before knocking on the door once again. After the third salvo Jock this time bade him come in. Ginger winked at Shepy and entered, closing the door quietly behind him.

Almost immediately he was back outside the door again.

"Fit happened?" asked Shepy incredulously.

"I shouldna'ive hin ma hans in ma pooches", Ginger groaned wearily.

The door-knocking ritual was repeated before he was called in. Now it was Shepy who put his ear to the door. He could scarcely hear Ginger plead his case, but there was no mistaking Jock's reaction. "You'll get your certificate at Prizegiving like everyone else and not before!" he snapped. "Now get out!" The door opened and a completely chastened, dispirited Ginger emerged. Without seeing, he

Hesitantly, Ginger turned the knob, eased open the door and peered in.

walked benumbed and dejected right past Shepy, who stood open-mouthed in the doorway.

"And what do you want?" Shepy suddenly realised that Jock was addressing him. He stepped tentatively into the room explaining his mission. Jock's demeanour instantly changed and horse-like teeth bared in his rendering of a smile – the first time Shepy could remember seeing this happen. The austere Central School head rarely smiled. He made a point of scrutinising all school report cards, generally dispersing them with a grunt. Those who fared badly in his pet subjects maths and science had their reports flung dismissively on the floor at their feet.

"Well done my boy. Well done." He now grinned hideously, looking more fearsome than ever as he beamed and handed over the envelope.

Back in class Shepy felt a glow of self-satisfaction and thanked his lucky stars he hadn't been in Ginger's shoes. His reverie was interrupted when he became aware Plookie was addressing Bill Milne and himself, her brows raised above saucer-like eyes.

"Well boys. You may now return my coins," she simpered. "I hope you found them interesting."

Reaching into their pockets each withdrew a handful of coppers and extracted French coins. Plookie noted several sous were missing. Pockets were turned out but no more sous were forthcoming. Shepy's and Bill's eyes met, then simultaneously it struck them. The North Kirk offering box!

"Please miss. We must have spent them by mistake." Plookie looked at them with disbelief. Then she began wringing her hands, bemoaning her loss.

"My precious coins. Oh you careless boys," she wailed. "C'est la guerre. France has capitulated. Those coins are irreplaceable."

Shepy tried to console his vexed teacher. "Please miss. Would you like some of my Japanese coins?"

Looking mortified Miss Adams placed her hands over her ears, rolled her eyes beseechingly roofwards and shrieked, "Say no more boy! Just say no more!" The class dissolved in laughter.

That night Shepy awakened when he smelt burning. Its source was traced to a small bin under his mother's bed in the kitchen recess. His savings stamps had not gone up in smoke nor were any sous found.

Just some dusters smouldering after her polishing the black-leaded iron grating whilst a fire was burning, but bringing home to Shepy in a way his arrant essay couldn't, the vital lesson to be learnt.

Loser in love and sport

A fierce spurt took him clear away from the others

THERE it was in the "Wizard" in black and white. Just the very tactics to use on school sports day. "Stay with the leaders of the pack," he read credulously, "accelerating on the last lap." Knowing the correct moment was all there was to it.

The tremendously popular comic paper character the amazing Wilson of the Wizard made the great Tarzan seem a mere also ran. In one episode the wonder athlete took a giant leap and broke the world long jump record while in the act of running a three-minute mile!

A game played by Shepy and schoolmates elevated Wilson to even greater achievements (if that were possible) than claimed in the popular weekly boy's paper.

Shepy: "Wilson climbed Mount Everest."

Kenny: "Bare fit."

Ping: "In blin' drift."

Tashy: "Blindfolded."

Shepy: "In half-an-hoor."

Kenny: "An army pack on his back."

Ping: "Walking backwards."

Tashy: "A tray o' bombs in each han'."

Athletics, like most sports, suffered during the war. There was no county cricket championship. Surrey's ground at the Oval was a prisoner-of-war camp. Wimbledon was a decontamination centre, Arsenal's ground at Highbury was a Civil Defence fortress, and golfers were few on the ground – courses being required for more urgent purposes.

The AAA championships, world records and the Olympics were all in limbo, just as in the 1914-18 war. There were no great athletes making headlines. They were all in the forces knocking recruits into shape.

Schools too, felt the pinch. Central School on Belmont Street – Schoolhill corner was requisitioned as a hospital. Pupils shared with Grammar School, half-days including Saturdays.

Junior school sports at Harlaw would be dominated by experienced third year boys like spring-heeled Jim Davidson, steadfast Joe Souttar and vigorous Percy Wray. But Shepy and classmates Kenny Thompson and Ping Ingram were not abashed. They had made it to the school soccer team, so they had to be in with a chance.

Impressing Cathy Wood also came into it as far as Shepy was concerned. A sturdy, sporting type, she played in the junior school hockey team and had completely captivated Shepy. So smitten was he that he'd sent her a note via Ping's sister Jenny.

A staunch fan of Shepy at Saturday morning football, the lissom Jenny, however, didn't figure in Shepy's thoughts in quite the same way as the buxom netball player.

Harlaw recreation grounds had a concrete-floored pavilion, spray baths and lockers under the dressing-room seats. The field was marked out for sprint events, high, long and triple jumps, etc. But the roped 440 yard circular track fascinated Shepy.

Third in the 100 yards behind Davidson and Thompson, and third in 220 yards, won by Souttar, Shepy felt he could only get better. Waiving three-legged and sack races which provided great amusement for the onlookers, he resorted to the obstacle race and again came third.

Between events he caught sight of Cathy Wood winning the girls 100 yards. Immaculate in utility fashion white top and snug black knickers, Shepy thought she looked divine. He wondered if she got his message.

Well into the proceedings came the main event for Shepy, the 440 yards. A large crowd gathered outside the pavilion where the finishing tape stretched across the track. Schoolmasters, natty Freddy Falconer and wheezy Chesty Fraser, sporting clipboards, scurried about lining up contestants.

The starter's shout could barely be heard above the roar of spectators cheering on their favourites, and they were off. Shepy kept abreast of the leaders as per plan, but was rather uneasy at the leisurely pace.

Nearing the halfway stage, Davidson broke ranks and surged ahead. This was not allowed for in Shepy's scheme. A bit confused, he opted to stay with the leaders of the pack as planned.

Reaching the last "pavilion" quarter, Shepy burst into action. A fierce spurt took him clear away from the others to gain swiftly on Davidson, some 30 yards ahead. With the crowd yelling encouragement for this sudden challenge, Shepy made his crucial sprint for the line and the gap closed rapidly.

Unable to increase his pace, Davidson's lead dissipated as Shepy hurtled round the bend into the home stretch, finally breasting the tape alongside his rival who was startled to be challenged in the last few strides of the race.

The last thing Messrs Falconer and Fraser wanted on their hands was an untidy dead-heat. Davidson, after all, had led for the entire race. So sadly for Shepy his scorching final bid was adjudged to have been just too late.

"Tough luck," they commiserated. "Hard cheese." Wallowing in the sympathetic back pats, Shepy felt elated – almost as if he had won. But it didn't last.

His great plan had come to grief. A furlong was no longer the maximum top-speed distance. He should have sprinted much more of the quarter-mile. And it didn't help, as he looked round, that Cathy Wood was nowhere to be seen.

The crowd melted away. There was no shot putt, discus or javelin in the junior sports. Throwing the cricket ball, the final event (for safety reasons), hadn't the same appeal.

But faithful Jenny kept a lonely vigil and watched him throw 74 yards to finish runner-up to Percy Wray. She caught up with him as he trudged wearily to the pavilion.

"Did ye give her the letter?" he asked forsakenly. She nodded. It was Jenny who waited when he emerged from the dressing room. Wordlessly they crossed Harlaw to the Cromwell Road gate and along to popular Giulianotti's cafe for a gassy vantas.

Runner-up athlete. Runner-up amorist. He bet Wilson of the Wizard never had this problem.

The humane race

... they arrived at the foot of the Patagonian Court steps...

"HONEST to God, I winna tell ony mair lees, I'll niver steal, swick or dae onything wrang. I'll finish my homework an' fitiver I'm telt. Cross my hairt and hope to die." Begging God's forgiveness, there was a note of desperation in Shepy's plaintive supplications.

It was Friday, and on the Brae, bespectacled secondary schoolboy Bob Insch had been flogging his tempting horse-racing tips for all he was worth. Bob had gained a reputation for picking winners. His technique was simple enough. Study form closely, isolate the likely winners and always quit when ahead.

Spreading his bets, he made up his own book and loved the war of wits between layers and backers. He knew all that was necessary about springers, long odds and short odds as well as the vagaries of the totalisator and each way accumulator.

The following day the Reiths, friends and former neighbours now living in the modern, prestigious, and much sought after Rosemount Square council development, were to travel with Shepy's parents to a funeral in Dundee. It was arranged that their small, red-haired son

Danny would be looked after by Shepy until they returned in the evening. Shepy's mother would leave plenty spam sandwiches, orangeade and clootie dumpling to tide them over.

This was okay with Shepy because previous occasions had yielded a generous halfcrown for his troubles – much less than a whole day. It was on the strength of this assumption he tried to lodge a bet. Bob, however, was not impressed.

"It's cash richt noo or naething!" he decreed, despite Shepy's voluble entreaties. But Shepy was not to be daunted. He knew that there was housekeeping money kept in a cocoa tin on the top shelf of the living room kitchen press, which only his father could reach without the help of a chair.

Biding his time till the coast was clear he climbed on the chair and opened the tin. There were some notes and coins. He snatched a halfcrown and duly placed his bet. They'd never know. After all, it was only a loan. As his parents and the Reiths said their goodbyes early on Saturday, Shepy was entrusted with the house key from his parents and given a parcel from the Reiths – for minding Danny they said. Immediately they'd gone it was ripped open to reveal an omnibus Greyfriars School Annual, featuring the inimitable Billy Bunter and friends. No money!

Shepy was mortified and rushed to the Brae to give Bob the news. There, the kids from around indulged in various activities to keep boredom at bay. Danny, who loved being involved in the outdoors was right in the middle of a football free-for-all with older kids, trying hard, but with not much success, to get a mere kick of the ball.

"Ken fit Eddie, I think I've been picked for my class team," he boasted as he ran hither and thither failing to make any contact whatsoever with the ball.

"Ye jist think it?" asked Shepy's bosom pal Eddie Munro.

"Well, it's nae official, but I heard the sports teacher say that if I wis in the team, I'd be a great drawback."

Eddie grinned, shaking his head in disbelief.

"Hey! Fit time wid it be aboot?", asked Danny, fast losing interest in the game.

"It's jist aifter one o'clock," replied Eddie.

"Is 'at a' it is?" Danny sounded disappointed. "It's usually later than 'at by this time."

Meanwhile Shepy was pursuing his case with Bob. "They aye gie me money," he remonstrated. "I wis expectin' a halfcrown. How wis I tae ken they'd gie me a bloomin' book?" The bet was off he said. "I jist canna tak' the risk. It's nae my money. I'll hae tae pit it back."

Bob gave him a glower. "Awa' an' flee up min. At's yer ain look oot, in't it?" he rasped. "It's a bittie late to cancel noo. I'm afraid ye've made yer bet!"

They continued arguing over the princely halfcrown bet, but Shepy was now looking uneasily around him.

"Far aboot's Danny gane?" he queried.

"I thocht you wis supposed to be watchin' him," Bob reminded him.

"Well he shouldna hive gane awa'. It's nae my fault," blurted Shepy full of guilt.

But to all intents and purposes Danny had disappeared from the Brae. Bob, feeling a bit responsible, began to muster a search party, gathering kids around him.

"Dis onybody hae ony idea far aboot he wid ging?"

Various suggestions were bandied about: Strachan's Gilcomston mill, Dunlop Rubber Co. depot, Kennerty Dairy bottling plant, Siddal & Hilton bedding factory, all close by. And the Denburn.

Aberdeen was well served by a number of burns: Howburn, Millburn, Westburn et al. But the greatest of these was the Denburn. There was something about it that fascinated the kids. Eddie recalled that Danny had been piqued at being left out of recent Denburn expeditions because of his tender age.

In the Rosemount area, at least, you hadn't earned your spurs until you had "dane the burnie", either paddling or wading according to the tides. Very few, however, had traced it through the dark culvert to the sea.

"That's it then," said Bob triumphantly. "It maun be the burnie. Danny'll be trying to prove himsel'."

Danny was indeed a lively, hyper-active eight-year-old who never seemed to tire. Finding him was proving no easy task. As time wore on, Bob, getting more anxious, kept them at it, hunting and searching, high and low, hoping to secure him safe and sound before his parents came home.

Shepy was in a right old pickle. He would never have "borrowed" and put at risk housekeeping money had he known he'd be rewarded with a book. And much worse, he seemed to have lost wee Danny.

During the intensive hue and cry covering every nook and corner of the Denburn, Bob softened up and benevolently returned Shepy's stake money from his own pocket. Shepy, gratefully relieved, sprinted home and restored it to the top shelf. He was back within minutes, in time to hear Eddie gloomily lament, "There's nae doot aboot it, if the tide's nae oot, he could be droont!"

The Denburn, flowing through the Grammar School grounds, under Esslemont Avenue and by culvert from Jack's Brae, by way of the valley of Union Terrace gardens and into the Harbour upper dock via the Joint Station, is sometimes tidal and prone to sudden flooding, so the observation was by no means wide of the mark.

After their arduous scour of the Denburn and every possible location in the neighbourhood, they arrived at the foot of the Patagonian Court steps on Denburn Road and wearily made the ascent to Belmont Street.

Conscience-stricken and full of remorse, Shepy prayed for deliverance and salvation. "Oh Lord," he blubbered, "Fit hiv I dane? Please forgive me and let us find Danny. I'll niver again ..."

"Hey! Haud yer weesht an' dicht yer snout. Dinna say nae mair!" Bob sucked in his breath. "I think I see the little beggar lookin' at the photies ootside the Belmont." The tired group shambled forward and bunched around him.

"Faur the heck hiv ye bin?" queried Bob. "We've bin lookin' a'wye fer ye!"

Danny, his blue eyes sparkling, suppressed a giggle. "I used mi sweetie money tae ging intae the Belmont. It wis a super Hopalong Cassidy Western." There could be no doubting the fact that this was one cinema where a kid could get in for the price of a powk of sweeties.

Languidly making their way home along the Viaduct, Bob purchased a Green Final. At Epsom, his horse, a rank outsider, had won by a whisker at good odds, and that cheered him up. Bob would also collect on Shepy's bet which had been too late to cancel, and his one shilling each way accumulator had built up to a goodly sum.

In a further gesture of magnanimity Bob gave Shepy another half-crown as a consolation, but reminded him: "Mak' up yer mind in future, and dinna iver dae 'at to me again. A bet's a bet ye ken."

Later, idly flicking through pages of the Greyfriars Annual, Shepy's eyes alighted on a story, "Billy Bunter's dead cert", with the Fat Owl himself coming to grief over a misplaced bet.

Hmm. Shepy could tell him a thing or two. Bob was a bit of a patter merchant, but fortunately a good-hearted bookie into the bargain.

Nae shorts at the school party

IT WAS a red letter day for Shepy. Getting a new suit was a major event for most, but in his case it meant something special. Clothing coupons presented no problem. More important was money, and Shepy had taken care of that.

Holidays were over. School was due back. Another year and he would be looking for a job. His old Rosemount pals had already left and were working. That's why he'd no hesitation taking a holiday job.

He badly missed out during the end of term Central School parties. At venues like Kennaway's or Empress Cafe, rooms were hired, scrambled dried egg, Spam sandwiches and surplus child welfare orange juice were dished up, with music provided by pupils. Boys and girls, segregated at school, got an opportunity to fraternise, dancing and participating in games considered daring if not quite licentious.

"Hey min, ye dinna ken fit yer missing," divulged classmate Bob Moodie, rolling his eyes lecherously. So far Shepy had given the parties a wide berth. To avoid getting involved he made excuses he was playing football, going to the pictures, couldn't be bothered with dames, or had a date with one!

"I've heard that song before," crooned sceptical Stanley Blackwell. Then suddenly for Shepy, earning some money became paramount. His career to date consisted of morning and evening newspaper rounds, and Saturday message bike deliveries for Cain the butcher up Rosemount. When the opportunity of a summer job arose after an upstair neighbour's chance remark to his mother, Shepy jumped at the chance although he had little idea what he was letting himself in for.

Alex Paterson, a stalwart toiling market gardener with a bushy Joe Stalin moustache, was offering an enticing 25 bob a week. His childless, house-proud wife Bella, constantly in hairnet and dustcap took great pride in their immaculately kept miniature backyard flower garden, a gorgeous profusion of blooms quite unmatched in the neighbourhood.

Often, a younger Shepy had been on the receiving end of her wrath as he retrieved (or tried to) balls from the luxuriant garden, overlooked from the second floor window where she kept regular watch. Her husband fared little better – banished to the backyard porch steps when he wanted a puff on his pipe.

Right on these steps one lunch hour during the first summer of the war, Mr. Paterson protectively pushed Shepy down behind him as a German Heinkel with three Spitfires on its tail flew directly overhead towards Ruthrieston. Crouched low, Shepy saw the action through his guardian's legs as the doomed bomber plunged earthwards to crash on the new ice rink on South Anderson Drive.

Mr. Paterson protectively pushed Shepy down behind him

Now, walking with his mother through the Co-op arcade in Loch Street towards the tailors and clothiers shop which also had a frontage on the Gallowgate, Shepy heaved a sigh of relief that he wasn't getting shoes. The boot and shoe department seats were overflowing as people queued outside.

Mind you the process of getting a suit wasn't particularly gratifying and thoughts about school party games did cross his mind. He imagined Hyde Park where boys sat in the dark with a lass on their knee while another lass roamed around with a torch, changing places with any girl caught kissing in the beam.

Popular were Postman's Knock and Bottly where the person in the middle of a circle spun a bottle and kissed the member of the opposite sex it pointed at when it stopped.

These too were the musings pervading his mind when, clad in an uncle in the force's bright-red, well-used boiler suit, with huge hems on sleeves and trousers taken up by his mother, he took the Dee/Don bridges tramcar, with distinct red band around its top deck, from the Junction to Crathie Terrace.

Nearby, in his plot on the old farm Outseats of Pitmuxton, in the Hardgate not far from the Holburn Street Railway Station, Alex Paterson grew flowers, fruit and vegetables to supply florists and grocers the length of Holburn and beyond.

Plenty weeding, digging for victory and picking berries had to be done and much of it fell to the unskilled Shepy. His co-workers were a scraggy old-timer and a brawny youth with a hairlip who reminded him of Will Hay's rumbustious partners Graham Moffat and Moore Marriott, but this pair knew their onions when it came to gardening.

Hauling the handcart up Holburn was the hardest part of the job. Juddering and jolting over the cassies, broad strap over one shoulder, hands clasped firmly on the shafts, on a hot day he neared exhaustion, while Mr. Paterson strode imperiously alongside on the pavement carrying order book under his arm.

At such moments Shepy knew what he was missing ... school belles Eva Smith, Isobel Fraser, Margaret Mundie and an exciting form of musical chairs. Boys on the chairs as the girls circled. What bliss when the music stopped!

He couldn't dance, but could pretend a bit to the music of classmates Doug Smith, devotee on trumpet, later Palais virtuoso, jocose Stan Allan on clarinet, budding Lothario Bob Moodie on piano and sparky Stanley Blackwell, son of ex-Dons goalkeeper, on drums.

Discarding such reflections for the one of himself in the shop mirror, Shepy rather liked the navy blue with fine red pinstripe. Labour economist Hugh Dalton had introduced utility clothing. Jackets were single-breasted and trouser turn-ups prohibited. Some tailors were prosecuted for disobeying and at a hostile press conference he was scathing. "There can be no equality of sacrifice in this war," he lamented. "Some lose lives and limbs, others only the turn-ups on their trousers."

Utility jokes proliferated. "Hiv ye heard aboot the utility chamber pot? Jist the sides are supplied. Ye pit in yer ain bottom!" or "Fit aboot a utility table? Bare legs and nae drawers!"

But Shepy loved his utility trousers. It was a milestone in his life. Other than the boiler suit it was his first suit with "langers", although he had only ever had one short-trouser suit!

His summer job had done it, with a bit extra to his mother to see them through. He felt greatly relieved he'd no longer have to dream up pretexts to escape school parties. Going in shorts he could never have contemplated. At last he had "langers" and could hardly wait for the next school party.

Son of a gun

"HEY MIN! Are you Phil Fowler fae Fonthill?"

"No," replied Shepy looking up in puzzlement at the bumptious cadet.

"Well I am," snapped the self-assertive youth, "an' yer lyin' in my place!"

Shepy gritted his teeth. Taking an instant dislike to the supercilious individual, he was deliberately unhurried getting to his feet, audibly muttering, "Fit difference dis it mak' onywye?"

Unconnected with the various visiting organisations, the burly resident NCO supervising the range noticed the incident and was on the spot instantly. He hastily ushered Shepy to another emplacement.

"At's fine ma loon. Y'see," he explained, "he aye tak's 'at position. Y'see. It's jist superstition."

While noting the hefty NCO punctuated all his sentences with "y'see", Shepy couldn't for the life of him see why Fowler or anyone else should get special preference. But he quickly dispelled the matter from his mind to concentrate on the event ahead.

"HEY MIN! Are you Phil Fowler fae Fonthill?"

Boys from the Grammar and Central schools were taking part in a marksmanship contest. To make it more exciting the NCO suggested each put a sixpence in a kitty to go to the winner. The youngsters were unanimous.

"At's jist hunky-dory," he beamed. "Y'see. It'll gar ye a' strive 'at bittie mair."

Shepy had been in the cadets only a few weeks. So many people were doing their bit these days. His father and most of his uncles were in the Services. Dave, an older uncle, was a founder member of the Local Defence Volunteers, now the Home Guard. Friends and neighbours did Civil Defence and Auxiliary Fire Service duties. Betty Keith was in the ATS, Beldie Cunningham was a Wren and Betty Buchan was in the Land Army. Kids he'd only recently played with were now in the Forces.

Anyway, with the Allies gradually getting the better of the Nazis in the war, Shepy just wanted in on the act to do his bit before it was all over.

Senior boys in the 16-18 group could get preliminary training for service in the local Home Guard companies, Sea Cadet and Air Training Corps. But wait! On reaching the age of 14 you could join the school Army Cadet Force where vacancies were quickly filled from a waiting list. Shepy knew his father didn't approve of boy soldiers but, in his absence, got his mother to sign the form. In khaki battle dress and forage cap, playground drill sessions and weapon training, field craft and map reading were tolerable, as were stripping down, cleaning and oiling the small-bore .22 calibre Lee-Enfield miniature replica rifle. He even pored earnestly over maths he disliked at school.

But the evenings spent training in the rudiments of marksmanship, shooting at printed targets, trying to place 10 consecutive shots into the tiny bullseye, at the indoor miniature rifle range in the Hardgate, were pure heaven as far as Shepy was concerned.

His introduction to the art was air-gun and pellets at Guestrow carnivals or Beach fairground arcades, father as tutor. So he was drawn to this fresh opportunity like a magnet and made quick progress.

Schoolmate Bill Milne was his main rival, but only on the shooting range were they evenly matched. Shepy's friendly challenger was a model cadet in every department, earning stripes in record time.

The contest entailed 10 shots each cadet, aimed from a prone position at a small target 50 feet distant. Competition was keen with "one-inch groups", "inners and outers" and "possible scores" part of the cadets' vocabulary.

The last cadet fired his last round and Shepy felt a tingle of excitement. It looked like Bill Milne and himself ahead of the field with little between them. He waited with bated breath.

"Cease fire! Bide faur ye are noo!" bellowed the NCO propelling his bulky frame down the aisle between the marksmen. "Y'see. Aince the scorin's coontit ..." He didn't finish the sentence as, after a quick, cursory glance over the targets, he snatched up Fowler's card, held it aloft and declared him winner.

There was a brief silence. Then came a chorus of questions and protests with Shepy and Bill Milne foremost. Raising his hands the NCO quietened them and began to expound.

"Y'see. It's nae aye the ane wi' the maist bulls fa wins. Raither, y'see. Fan mair hit the card fit ye've tae tak' intae accoont is, ah, oh, er, well ... y'see."

Shepy didn't see at all and later, still unconvinced, tackled a Grammar schoolboy of his acquaintance outside.

"I dinna think 'at guy o' yours won ava."

"Neither do I," replied the other lad raising his eyebrows. "But he's not ours. We thought he was yours."

It was some time after Shepy learnt that Fowler was a regular at Fonthill Barracks. Planted among raw cadets, youthful looks rendered him inconspicuous, and competent shooting, extricated by waffle on occasion, paid off in a split with the unprincipled NCO.

Nae winner they ran a kitty, Shepy thought. What a stingy way of doing their bit!

Turning a blind eye?

THE corridor walls were lined with framed pictures of winning cricket, rugby and hockey teams of years gone by. There was little emphasis on soccer, but one captured Shepy's interest, causing pause in his stride: the shield-winning school football team of 1927.

Now, 18 years on, he studied the youngster in the front row, George Mutch. A schoolboy international, this former pupil, in the season prior to the war clinched the FA cup for Preston North End from the penalty spot against Huddersfield with the last kick of extra time, and was a member of the Scottish side which triumphed over England at Wembley.

Scarcely daring to dream of such heady success, Shepy's lesser ambition was to join the picture gallery in a contemporary team photograph. Up there on the wall with the others, a sort of hall of fame, viewed with curiosity by succeeding generations of pupils, perhaps posthumous respect in course of time, immortality of a kind.

And he fancied he'd made it. Winning through to the school trophy final; smartly turned out in new dark blue strip replacing customary Central School green; the inimitable Peter Craigmyle as referee; and the thrill of a lifetime playing at Pittodrie before a crowd.

Shepy's father, now a leading aircraftsman, was sometime member of his RAF unit football eleven (by the skin of his teeth, he admitted), and had won an inter-command competition. In his squad were Neil Franklin, Stoke City and England centre-half, and Jackie Oakes, Queen of the South winger and Powderhall sprinter.

This impressed Shepy no end and had the effect of firing him to emulate his dad's success in the final against conquering new school Powis. Future Dons Ken Thompson, Billy Smith and Jim Wallace were in Central's ranks to face shield-holders Powis, boasting senior-bound Davie Aitken (Dons), Jim Chalmers (Queen's Park) and Jack Kirby (Stoke City).

Hopes soared when Central took an early lead through speedy winger "Toochie". But Shepy's dream was not to be. Aitken equalised for Powis and, after a bitter struggle, Chalmers netted a penalty in the dying seconds of the game.

Broken-hearted, Shepy could not hide his tears in the sanctuary of the dressing-room. There would be no victorious team picture on the corridor wall. It was some time before he got over the disappointment.

But that was last season. Now he was even more optimistic than before. New sports master, his register teacher, easy-going, bluff "Chesty" Fraser made him captain of the school soccer team, winners of the league championship.

With a useful nucleus of "left-overs" from the previous term, including Wallace, Smith and classmate "Ping" Ingram, Central were now set on achieving the double by winning the shield knock-out competition. In the semi they met arch-enemies Powis. A chance to wreak revenge.

Played on the big pitch at Harlaw, in front of the pavilion, this match was watched by an enthusiastic crowd and some juvenile scouts. Revenge was sweet. Playing with style they trounced hapless Powis 4-0. Manfully working for the opposition was "Toochie" who hadn't quite settled at Central and now found himself up against his old mates. Again Shepy dreamt of glory to come at Pittodrie second time round.

Chesty wheezed delight just like when he won at chess. Almost as important as his stewardship of the school team was his great love of chess. During intervals and odd opportunities he would play Shepy's classmate Ian "Slinky" Middleton.

Mediocre at football but a future Scottish boy chess champion, Middleton yearned in vain to make the football team. Shepy would have settled for playing football as well as Slinky played chess. Chesty settled for giving the prodigy a good game.

When the bubble burst Chesty was caught napping. Was it an oversight? Perhaps he didn't want to know. The typed message on the school notice board was brief, terse and final.

"Due to a registration discrepancy the school has scratched from the shield competition. (signed) John W. Robertson, MA, BSc, headmaster."

Responsibility for checking age eligibility lay with the sports master. There was very little in it. There never is. But unfortunately, intake and leaving dates at junior and secondary schools differed, and apparently he had shut his eyes to it. Nevertheless, Shepy and Ping had definitely erred, letting down the school and their teammates.

Ex-players in the upper school assured the wretched pair that their deed was commonplace, but rarely a subject for complaint. Poor prejudged Toochie was cast in the role of clype as his mentor, Powis sportsmaster and Aberdeen FC director Charlie Forbes, pursued a hat-trick of shield victories.

Although millions were celebrating the sordid suicide of Hitler, Shepy was inconsolable. Despite his signing for a juvenile club; Powis losing to Frederick Street School in the final; Germany's surrender; victory in Europe and an end to the war in sight – all gladsome news – yet his dream of appearing in a team photograph on the corridor wall was well and truly scuppered.

Sporting records were suspended and didn't count for much during the war. His vain photo whimsy was a fallacy from the start. The exigencies of war put paid to that novelty along with class pictures, school magazine and other niceties. But Shepy took a while to get it out of his system that, unwittingly or not, his failure to observe the rules was to blame.

Nessun dorma – barrin' Billy

He slept peacefully through the entire second half

IT was just like Charlie Chaplin in Modern Times. The little team of two men and two boys worked steadily through the forenoon, sorting the crate mountain of empties being fed through the conveyor belt, separating Alexander's, Robertson's, Sang's, Thompson's and odd outside-town aerated water firms, from William Hay & Sons' own bottles.

Snatching the glass necks between nimble fingers, Shepy was becoming quite expert at identifying the different bottles in the endless flow, before slotting them into the appropriate box. It did, however, become boring after a spell, and he looked forward to the mid-morning break.

Even so, the nature of the work at least left his mind fairly free to wander, and he was agog, full of anticipation, expectancy and excitement.

The day before, he and bottle-sorting partner little Billy Adams heard the ominous, on-the-prowl clink-clink of Sinclair Milne's calliper-boot, and kept their heads down in a show of industry designed to ingratiate themselves with the no-nonsense assistant manager.

Shortly after starting at Hay's, Shepy had been initiated in the time-honoured tradition – dumped unceremoniously in the dung heap, then thrown into the horse trough. There was no malice. Indeed, two perpetrators dried him out in the boiler house. Mr. Milne disapproved such behaviour. What was it now?

He came, however, bearing two complementary tickets, circle seats in HM Theatre for the matinee performance of La Traviata. They had gone the round of office hierarchy without takers; drivers who'd shown no interest; offered ultimately, since no one else appeared to want them, to the two youngest employees.

Philistines all, thought Shepy, put on his beam-ends at first, when Billy said he'd never heard of it, but would go just to get Wednesday afternoon off.

At every opportunity since, Shepy had been humming familiar bits, desperately trying to impress the wee lad, but without much success.

"Listen," he cajoled Billy before launching into a rendering of "*Hear My Song, Violetta*". "They pinched 'at ye ken," he railed indignantly. "*The prelude to Act 1.*" The usually chirpy wee chap nodded glumly as Shepy insisted on tra-la-la-ing *Brindisi* and *Sempre Libera*, and must have been grateful for the whistle heralding the break.

This was taken alongside the bottle-sorting line, where they sat on upturned boxes. As usual, genial old-timer Bob Esson, charge-hand of the group, sat on his cushion, opened his tea flask and unwrapped his sandwich. His deputy Albert, a handicapped person with the strength of an ox and the two youngsters enjoyed Bendy Low pies, fetched in by the van boy from popular pastry baker Jessamine in Causewayend.

Gulped down with choice of orange, lime or lemonade splits, the marvellous rule was that all you desired could be consumed on the premises. Only Pepsi-cola was under lock and key – for sole benefit of US servicemen.

"Fan did this musical first come oot, onywye?" queried Billy.

"Oh, a good whiley ago," replied Shepy. "It's based on Dumas' The Lady of the Camelias. There's drinkin', gamblin', scandal, high-class courtesans an' a'thing," he divulged knowledgeably, having read the crit in the previous night's Evening Express.

"Fit's courtesans?"

"Prostitutes."

"Oh! Well! Mmmm ..." Billy pondered.

But it was soon back to the conveyor belt. There was, of course, more to the job than sorting bottles. A great diversion was riding the lorry transporting crates of these very bottles to the Bottle Exchange Depot in Nelson Street, swapping for Hay's bottles deposited by other companies.

Just opposite the depot was the old Globe Picture Playhouse, used as a services training centre during the war. Shepy heard all about "Globie" jam-jar admittance and wondered how many would get in for a box of lemonade empties?

Through in the factory bottling section, manned mainly by women, bottles were filled, stoppered, labelled and crated. Another chore was ferrying the crates to the store. Stacking the top shelf had him painfully stretched on tiptoe, teetering and wavering precariously, attempting to lodge the crate.

At mid-day most of the factory went home for lunch. Home and Hay's, about a mile apart as the crow flies, saw Shepy trot short-cuts between Berryden and Northfield in a few minutes, to catch the canteen entertainment of Workers Playtime and stirring overtures to Lunch Hour Concerts on the radio.

Getting this job in the first place hadn't been easy. Well, perhaps getting the job was easy enough, but persuading his mother to sign the school leaving form had been difficult. He would never have got away with it if his father had been demobbed. Encouraged to stay on for higher education Shepy demurred, witlessly reasoning that his pals were working and that somehow he was getting one over on "heidy" Jock Robertson.

"Laddie," his granny said, "fit ye need to get on in life is a gweed education, a gweed job and a gweed wife." The latter was some way off, and he needed to keep working on the others. But what of aesthetic things? Well, Verdi's masterpiece was peppered with great tunes but, opera didn't suit everyone.

The first act held Billy's attention. After that he was very restless until the interval, when he appeared to revive, looking around and enjoying Donald's ice cream. But from there on he slept peacefully through the entire second half outpouring of beautiful, poignant melody.

The applause at the finale woke him up. Looking at Shepy, now on his feet clapping madly, as if he was a born sucker, the wee fella, suitably refreshed, made a confident prophecy.

"See 'at show. Well, I'll tell ye this much. It'll niver be a hit!"

Lost leader

SITTING straight in the saddle, Wild Bill Hickock rode slowly down the steep stage road and pulled up. He pushed his stetson to the back of his head, mopped his brow and surveyed the wide prairie before him. Reining in his horse, he nervously fingered the butt of the Colt '45 in his belt.

Suddenly he swung round, pulled his hat down hard and galloped off down the trail, signalling his scouting party to follow and furiously leather-whipping the flanks of his mount. There was no time to lose. There were Red Indians out there!

Not for nothing had Moshie been dubbed "king o' the kids".

In the way that a person's life is said to pass before their eyes when drowning, this typical, gung-ho reincarnation, enacted on Jack's Brae, had raced through Shepy's mind as he read the disturbing report in the paper. He was stunned at the news, but it must have been correct because there it was in the Evening Express for all to see.

It was scarcely a couple of weeks since they all had a good laugh, learning that Moshie's mother had written to the Naval Training Department complaining that her son never wrote home. Poor Moshie would still have been trying to live down his embarrassment at being summoned before his commanding officer and lectured about his duty to write home. Further instructed to bring the letter to the officer so he could ensure it was posted, only added to his humiliation.

But now had come this devastating news...

Not for nothing had Moshie been dubbed "king o' the kids". But past-master though he was in the field of popular street games, it was not for that attribute alone had he achieved renown.

Something of a "Pied Piper o' Jack's Brae" to the younger kids, he sought to bring to life their heroes, as he became Robin Hood, General Custer, Gary Cooper, Buffalo Bill, Errol Flynn, Monty or Captain Scott – hero and film star frequently juxtaposed.

In turn, the kids were his merry men, cavalry, legionnaires, posse, or just poor bloody infantry. The Brae was transformed into Sherwood Forest, Little Bighorn, Tunisian Desert, Wild West, Balaclava, No Man's Land, complete with real trenches, and even the Antarctic when the Brae became snowbound in winter.

His repertoire of games and ideas was inexhaustible and there was rarely a dull moment. Moshie was virtually an unpaid youth leader providing far more excitement than the Cubs or Life Boys.

Perhaps his greatest coup was the organised forays into the nearby West End, scrauning the buckets and sharing the spoils with his impecunious young followers.

Moshie was, like Peter Pan, a boy who just wouldn't grow up. Yule the grocer, whose shop was just across the road, had a sympathetic ear.

"I ken some o' the ithers tak' me for a chump 'cos I've aye played wi' the kids," confided Moshie. "Oh, er, gi'es half-a-stane o' tatties."

"It's a dampt shame, so it is, consoled the grocer. "But niver mind. I'll gie ye sma' anes, so they'll nae be so heavy to cairry hame."

Poor Moshie missed the joke, as so often he did. And he continued to endure a good deal of ribbing and leg-pulling from the lads his own age who were, naturally, somewhat bored with mere children.

Finding it difficult to get a steady job, he became more or less self-employed when taking on several newspaper rounds, and farming out deliveries among the willing kids before and after school every day. He paid them in coppers for their labour and, in true business fashion, creamed off a fair profit for himself.

"Y're nae feart takin' a len o' the kids the wye that ye dae?" chivvied Dod Gibson, learning of Moshie's opportunism.

"I dinna ken the meaning o' fear," retorted Moshie, drawing himself up to his full height in a fair rendition of the Lone Ranger.

"Well, ye can aye look it up in the dictionary," replied Dod with a straight face.

Moshie then took a big step in his desire to earn an honest penny. He revealed genuine entrepreneurial skills in persuading a wholesale newsagent supply depot behind The Tivoli Theatre to supply him with surplus, past their publication date, John Bull, Everybody's, Picture Post, Illustrated, Answers and Tit-bits magazines, at greatly reduced prices. He then sold them at cut-price terms to doctors, dentists, solicitors, architects and hairdressers – any business in the wider Rosemount area with a waiting room.

But his days at the top were numbered. The kids of his era, his stock-in-trade, were now finishing school and moving on to new things. He was getting just too old as, inevitably, the age gap ever widened between himself and the next crop of youngsters coming up. It was time for something new, and so it was he joined the navy, enrolled at the Royal Naval College at Greenwich.

He was a big lad and, on his first leave in uniform, was much admired by his ex-followers. But in truth he was in deep waters, experiencing trouble in adjusting and settling down. He found things a lot different in the navy, and difficulties in getting on with the lads in the same age group as himself.

Time didn't stand still and perhaps Moshie couldn't face growing up. He had grown into, if not quite grown up to be, a young man. He was certainly no brainbox, but neither was he as thick as two planks.

Not surprisingly, however, he received little respect from his peers at sea, and was picked on and targeted by naval officers requiring cannon fodder to ram home their cautionary tales.

Now he was gone, and his loss at sea was a complete mystery. Did he fall, was he pushed, or did he jump? Rumours were rife. Could it have been unrequited love? Young men and boys often found it difficult to talk about their problems and relationships. He was a powerful swimmer. Perhaps he just swam away from it all?

Shepy's eyes returned to the sombre piece in the newspaper, "...naval cadet on HMS Ganges at Harwich missing, believed drowned...presumption of death, accident or misadventure...no suspicious circumstances." The coroner recorded an open verdict.

So that was it. Moshie had vanished without trace. Well he may not have realised it, but when the dauntless leader became "king o' the kids" he also became, in his own small way, a legend. With his own brand of swashbuckling derring-do he brought the kids real, live and exhilarating action – and they loved every minute.

You can't do much better than that.

Miss MacDonald's double

"I'll bet that's a Jowett."

"SEE! I telt ye," crowed Billy Adams. "It's a Wolseley."

"Gosh! Gee! Yuh don't say!" gulped Bob Sutter in an uncanny impersonation of Goofy, the lugubrious Disney character.

The volume of cars on the roads was still such as to make identification an enjoyable pastime. Shepy, ensconced between the lively pair in the cab of a Bedford lorry, absently beheld Billy pinpoint every model that passed – Hillman or Humber, Rover or Riley, Singer or Sunbeam.

Requiring a good sighting of bonnet mascot or radiator badge to be certain, Shepy was beaten to it time and again. But right now his mind was elsewhere and his performance showed it. He had discovered Jeanette MacDonald.

After two visits to the Cinema House, sitting through Rose Marie twice round each time, he had fallen head over heels in love with the attractive singing star. Her concern for errant brother James Stewart, between love songs with Nelson Eddy and stage duets with Allan Jones, was a mellifluous concoction that had won him over completely.

Shepy much preferred travelling about town to being cooped up inside Hay's lemonade depot. He had moved on from bottle-sorting to unloading vehicles in the yard, but had been glad to get away from that.

Popular gaffer Jim McBain was paid off when his predecessor Corporal Armstrong, built like Don Emery, was demobbed. Acting like he was still in the army, he bullied younger lads, delighting in delaying work until the last minute, then keeping them behind to clear the decks before leaving.

It was another world out there on the Albion, Bedford and chain-driven Thorneycroft lorries, delivering orders to pubs, clubs, hotels and restaurants; or on horse and cart, with towering load up behind, doing some hard selling round the shops.

This way he got to know other van boys. Billy's older brother Sonny and worldly Les Cassie had an eye for the girls. Listening credulously to their philandering exploits, Shepy envied their apparent arrival at a stage he was still thinking about.

Built to hold 800 skaters and regarded a likely place to "get off your mark", Donald's Ice Rink in Spring Garden was a popular rendezvous of Hay's van boys. There, novice skater Shepy garnered a lot more talk than action. He would bide his time.

Worthy, long-serving carters at Hay's loved and groomed their magnificent horses regularly. But amongst the lorry drivers, a more transitory species, favourite with the youngsters was Bob Sutter. Only a few years older than his van boys, he brooked no nonsense. Tuned effortlessly into their wavelength, however, his good-natured banter, Disney character mimicry and endless supply of sweeties ensured loyalty and respect.

Parking outside spirit merchant Argo in George Street, they delivered bottled drinks, precious soda siphons and potato crisp ration, packed in tins and in short supply, before returning to the cab leaving Bob to settle up with the customer. After a few minutes Billy nudged Shepy.

"C'mon let's hae a gander roon' the Rubber Shop windaes."

Formerly in St Nicholas Street, opposite Raggie Morrisons, the brand new shop featured a modern stroll-around frontage with elegant window displays. Cavalierly glossing over the exhibits, Shepy's eyes widened as they alighted on a postcard size picture frame.

He stood transfixed. His heart melted. There in the window, with a simply adorable, irresistible smile was his screen goddess, Jeanette MacDonald.

Shepy's longing was sublime. He had to have her. Suddenly he was in the shop expressing his desire to a young assistant.

"I don't really want the frame," he apologised sheepishly, "It's just the picture I'm interested in." She smiled encouragingly, saying she'd find out.

Billy caught up to be enlightened by the time the girl returned to say she'd remove it from the frame and bring it in a moment. Shepy now studied her very closely.

"Ken this," he whispered earnestly, "she looks like Jeanette MacDonald."

"Ye think so?" countered Billy dubiously.

"Same hair, same eyes, same nose, same mouth," breathed Shepy.

"Hey! Can ye sing?" asked Billy cheekily when the girl returned. "He thinks ye're like Jeanette MacDonald."

Handing the picture to Shepy she smiled prettily. The earth must have moved then, for acting on a sudden impulse, and in as deep a voice as he could muster, Shepy blurted out, "Would you care to go to the pictures with me on Saturday night?"

The few moments pause while she gave it some thought seemed an eternity to Shepy. "That would be nice," she decided with a smile. "Where shall we meet?"

There was some explaining to do when they returned to the lorry. Bob was drumming his fingers impatiently on the wheel.

"Faur the heck hiv ye bin a' this time?" he demanded.

Billy explained. Shepy blushed. Bob just laughed. Eyebrows raised in mock wonder, he quacked in his best Donald Duck, "OK lover boy! Let's get goin'!" The news would be sure to travel fast in Hay's, doing Shepy's standing no harm.

Driving off, Billy was already at the window. "I'll bet that's a Jowett." Then, as it passed, adding, "Yup. I telt ye."

Shepy sank back luxuriously on the seat. He wasn't seeing. He wasn't hearing. He had just made a date with Jeanette MacDonald's double and was feeling pretty pleased with himself.

Dynamo in a stew!

Bill had come across a low-priced cafe in nearby King Street

SHEPY tasted the stew. It was thick and mouth-watering, with just the right touch of seasoning to tickle the palate. But …

From the moment he started work bottle sorting that day, all talk had been about the big match due at Ibrox Stadium between Rangers and Moscow Dynamo. The Russian visitors had been showing the British sides a thing or two, defeating Arsenal and Cardiff, the latter 10-1!

Aberdeen had tried to fix up a match with the USSR team, but without success. So the radio broadcast of the game in the afternoon was as close as Shepy would ever get to Dynamo.

During the break the debate continued with “bit of a know-all driver” Bill Bennett claiming vociferously that Rangers players of his day, notably Meiklejohn, McPhail and Morton, would have wiped the floor with Dynamo. But all too soon their brief respite was over and it was back to the monotony of the conveyor belt for some, with the subject unresolved.

The crates of rival firms' sorted bottles were transported by lorry to the Bottle Exchange Depot in Nelson Street, to be traded for Hay's bottles which had been deposited there by other companies.

On the trip, Bill was accompanied by his second man, 18-year-old Les Cassie and stand-in Shepy, both of whom eulogised the prowess of the Glasgow club's present day players, and were Rangers supporters for the day.

The war had been over for just a few weeks, but already eating places were popping up all over the place. On his rounds, Bill had come across a low-priced cafe in nearby King Street, and enthusiastically recommended their speciality, Irish Stew, to his young hands.

Shepy usually had lunch at home, taking sandwiches if he knew he would be out on a lorry. He quickly succumbed, however, when Bill offered to pay, having collected a handsome bonus, "by virtue of his salesmanship" as the certificate put it.

"Ay, virtue is its ain reward," Bill crowed the familiar platitude as his young crew expressed their thanks.

"But dae ye really get onything extra for being virtuous?" sniffed Les.

"Listen. Ye dinna get well-peyed fer working hard onywye," confided Bill. "Effort on its ain is nae aneuch. It's achievement and producing results fit coont." He went on, "If it wis jist a maitter o' hard graft, then manual labourers wid mak' much mair siller."

The place was fairly crowded, but they secured a table next to the kitchen, and soon were tucking into a scrumptious concoction of mutton, potatoes and onions, swimming in a rich, spicy gravy.

Thoroughly enjoying his stew, garrulous Bill became loquacious once more about the Rangers team when he was a youngster. Shepy only half heard, having become totally distracted by goings on in the kitchen. Directly opposite, he could see the stewing in a huge cauldron, and staff sweeping the leavings on plates back into the cauldron.

He nudged Bill and motioned surreptitiously with his eyes towards the kitchen. The driver just looked, laughed and shrugged.

"*Ashes to ashes, dust to dust.*
If a bomb disnae get me
This Irish stew must!"

Just then an elderly gent shuffled in the door. Wiping the back of his hand across his nose, he ambled up to their table and sank down heavily on the remaining seat. In a spontaneous surge of benevolence, Bill invited him to have a plate of stew at his expense, and within minutes the old man was golloping his stew noisily while listening intently to the exchanges on the merits of players of different generations.

Bill turned towards him fully expecting support, but none was forthcoming from the old codger who had his own ideas on the subject. Between copious mouthfuls he soon made clear his allegiances, and a Rangers supporter he was not! Becoming quite heated he criticised the Glasgow club past and present, with considerable venom for an old stager, and Bill and he kept at it, first one pontificating while the other butted in.

"Calm doon min! Calm doon!" remonstrated Bill, his patience stretched to the limit. "Ye'll burst yer gizunker if ye cairry on like this."

"I'll remind ye," slobbered the old-timer vehemently, the gravy dribbling down the sides of his mouth, "that efter winnin' the cup in 1903, Rangers niver won it again until 1928 – that wis 25 years withoot winnin' the cup!"

"But fit aboot R.S. McColl, ye aul foggie?" countered the well-read Hay's driver, referring to the Queen's Park and Rangers star who made his international debut at 19, scored three hat-tricks in five internationals at the turn of the century, and earned the title "Prince of centre-forwards".

"Toffee Bob, fa?" spluttered the old geezer. "He wis better aff selling sweeties," adding spitefully, "I hope the Ruskies beat 'em!"

With that he belched uncontrollably, his false teeth spewed from his mouth and disappeared from sight, buried in his stew, and splashing the food, faces and clothes of all at the table.

"Fit a sotter! At's put me richt aff me denner!" squirmed Bill. "An' at's a' the thanks ye get."

This effectively ended the debate, and departure soon followed. But it took a new turn on the road back to Hay's as Les and Shepy let poor Bill have it.

"Far aboot will ye get a team wi' better defenders than Young, Shaw and Woodburn?" queried Les. "It's nae picnic trying to score against them."

"At's richt," parroted Shepy. "And Waddell, Thornton and Duncanson will tak' them apart." But Bill would brook no argument, just shook his head and concentrated on the drive back to Berryden.

Later in the afternoon after their return, they and many other employees kept up with the game, making canny visits to the office. There, a radio which had kept staff informed of the progress of the war was now broadcasting the progress of a football match.

The news passed round the factory by word of mouth, and soon it was apparent that before a 90,000 crowd, Rangers were 2-0 down. It seemed all over bar the shouting, and something of an anti-climax.

But no! Rangers were not to be outdone as they snatched a creditable draw in a great fight against Dynamo who caused a furore regarding substitutes by having twelve men on the field for a spell, and who were in fact a Russian national team.

The cafe on King Street? Well yes, there had been a war on and the Irish stew wasn't that bad – although Bill should have been made to eat some of his words. Les and Shepy figured the cantankerous old beggar must have been a communist.

Needless to say, after the dogged old chap's false teeth mishap, Shepy never returned to that somewhat niggardly establishment, which to put it mildly had been over-economical with the stew.

Keep smiling through

A tiny, spruce man with serious eyes and walrus moustache, Mr. Charles was always immaculate

IT WAS Ina Charles who suggested it to Shepy's mother. Ina and her dad worked for Averys in King Street and she said she'd get him to put in a word.

Shepy had already shrugged off prospects of newspaper work via a great-uncle with influential position in the Broad Street despatch department. He wanted to get a job off his own bat and in any case didn't much fancy despatch.

Living in the same tenement as Mr. Charles, it would have been discourteous not to acknowledge the offer. So Shepy was urged to listen and do what he was told.

Aberdeen was chock-a-block with printers. He had submitted his name to half-a-dozen in the Belmont Street, Market Street area alone. One more would make little difference.

A tiny, spruce man with serious eyes and walrus moustache, Mr. Charles was always immaculate. In dark suit, starched collar and tie, bowler hat and gleaming dress boots, he walked smartly to and from work daily. Shepy was certain he was manager.

Proudly, Mr. Charles enlightened him of Avery's history. Known as Greyfriars Press, the firm had been on the go for over 100 years, from beginnings in the Gallowgate before moving to King Street in 1892, and boasted HM Stationers Office among many esteemed customers.

His advice seemed all too obvious to Shepy. Get a haircut, wear his best suit, keep hands out of pockets and make sure shoes were polished. There was more. He should stand up straight, keep shoulders well back, and speak in a clear voice, addressing the boss, Mr. Youngson, as sir.

"Be positive. Come richt oot and say you've come for a job, and how much you would like to work at Avery's," lectured Mr. Charles. "Dinna mumble or hum an' ha aboot if he needs any apprentices. He canna stan' that. Got that now?" Shepy nodded and was going over it in his mind when his mentor said there was one last thing.

"Fit's 'at?" asked Shepy feebly.

"A big smile," said Mr. Charles. "He disnae like lang faces either."

After a busy week practising his spiel and trying out various smiles, Saturday morning found Shepy nearing Avery's doing a final rehearsal. Acting out every hint and wrinkle he could remember, shoulders back, mouthing platitudes and baring teeth in an inane smile, he collided with a big, grey-haired, bespectacled man he hadn't noticed pausing in the entrance way, treading on his toes for good measure.

Giving the embarrassed Shepy a funny look, the man proceeded across Mealmarket Street to the Bank. Shepy hurried in and asked the first person he saw for directions to Mr. Youngson's office.

"Jist go straight through. Ye'll see the door. Mind an' knock." he was told.

Skirting the machine-room, Shepy experienced another jolt. Clad in ink-stained boiler suit, at full stretch over a flat bed cylinder machine doing "make-ready", was his immaculate Mr. Charles.

Reaching the door, Shepy knocked firmly and waited. After a pause, he knocked again, shouting, "May I come in, sir?"

There was another pause, followed by a voice from within. "Well ... hold on ... just a sec." Then came the unmistakable swooshing sound of a toilet being flushed. The door opened. Out stepped a man in waistcoat and fob watch and chain.

Embarrassed once more, Shepy kept his head and beamed. "Excuse me, sir. I've come for a job. It has always been my wish to work for

Avery's."

"Hold on son. You want Mr. Youngson." The man pointed. "Try over there. Mind to knock."

There seemed no end to Shepy's embarrassment. Gathering himself together, he strode to the door indicated and knocked.

"Come in," called a voice. Shepy entered to be confronted by a slim, mild-looking, elderly man standing in front of a desk laden with books, leaflets and folders. Forcing a huge smile, he tried again.

"Good morning, sir."

"Good morning, laddie," the man replied warmly. Shepy relaxed. This wasn't the ogre he had expected.

"I've come about a job. I've always wanted to work at Avery's." Certain the man was impressed, he surged on. "When would you like me to start?" Shepy waited expectantly.

"I don't know. I can't really say. You better wait for Mr. Youngson." The old chap's weathered face softened into a self-deprecating smile. "I'm only the porter-messenger here."

Shepy's heart sank into his stomach. His shoulders sagged. His smile evaporated. He felt miserable. He looked miserable.

Suddenly the door opened and a big, grey-haired, bespectacled man entered. "Here you are George," he said, handing a package to the porter-messenger, who muttered in reply, "Right, Mr. Youngson," and shuffled out with a sympathetic glance towards Shepy.

It was the man in the collision at the entrance. Fixing Shepy, now apprehensive, with a baleful look, he demanded, "And what are you after?"

"D-do y-ye n-need any apprentices?" mumbled Shepy with no hint of a smile.

He never heard any more from Avery's. Having cast his net wide, however, he did get a promising postcard from James Blair in Market Street. That is another story.

Shepy's hapless hero

"FIT'S the name o' this aul street?" asked Ian Sanders. Shepy's head twisted in all directions until his eyes lit on a grimy, barely discernible sign fixed high on the drab, sombre building.

"Sandyfaulds Street," he replied.

It was, indeed, an old begrimed street, but Shepy, instilled with a sense of excitement and adventure, was savouring every moment of his first visit to Glasgow, even as they wandered, in fading light, ever deeper among grim-like, forbidding buildings under the tolerantly-amused gaze of the long-suffering locals.

Thanks to an old Rosemount School classmate Ian Sanders, now a bookbinder apprentice with Rose Street printers Middletons and a staunch Dons supporter, Shepy had got a seat on their bus, bound for the final of the first-ever League Cup tournament. The journey south had taken him through places he'd only heard of, to arrive at the most distant point to which he had ever travelled.

Only one thing about the whole business disappointed him, and that was the abrupt dropping of one of his footballing heroes from the team for the final. Exempt from war service due to his work in the shipyards, Jock Pattillo had broken goal-scoring records left, right and centre. This was shabby treatment for his efforts.

At the match, played on Hampden Park before 135,000 spectators, all was forgiven and forgotten. Another of his favourites, George Taylor, scored the winner for a Dons team featuring Willie Cooper, Frank Dunlop, George Hamilton, Stan Williams and Archie Baird, that defeated a strong Rangers side containing Duggie Gray, Tiger Shaw, George Young, Scott Symon, Willie Waddell and Willie Thornton, by 3-2.

Celebrating with a slap-up tea in a Buchanan Street restaurant, the youngsters listened avidly as Middleton's soccer buffs Alex Brown, Jim Marr and Archie Mutch elaborated on the finer points of the game before departing to a nearby pub, telling the youngsters to stay in the vicinity till they got back.

With no guide and not a lot of time, there was no chance of city sight-seeing. Going on a victory stroll seemed like a good idea. Sporting their red favours, they started off along Buchanan Street keeping a fairly straight furrow so as to simplify their way back.

Jubilant Ian wore his red wollen toorie bonnet at a jaunty angle while Shepy, his dad's old black and gold scarf no longer appropriate, had been rescued by his mother with the strip of red flannel now draped nattily around his neck. Apart from odd looks from kids their own age, the odyssey passed without incident.

Crossing Argyle Street and nearing the Clyde, they passed a printing works, reminding Shepy he was due to start with a printing firm the following week, albeit only as a messenger boy. At that precise moment responsibilities seemed to weigh heavily on his shoulders.

With football training two nights per week and enroled in advance for evening classes at Marywell Street School of Printing three evenings per week, notwithstanding infrequent escorting home girl students from the hair-dressing class in the same building, there was little time for much else – especially going steady.

The harmonious liaison with Violet, the Rubber Shop assistant he had befriended, suffered as a result. They had hit it off in many ways, enjoying pleasant times at the City Cinema and Grand Central, a stonethrow from her home in Farquhar Place, a tiny enclave off the Gallowgate. This outing, however, on top of everything else, could be the last straw.

Major commitments so early in life, so severely constricting, are not for the free-spirited. Shepy felt trapped at a time he was about to make a fresh start – a new beginning in print. Sadly, it appeared to be a classic example of the right people having met at the wrong time.

He would also learn that fate played some funny games. Unfortunate in that his best footballing years coincided with World War II, his idol Jock Pattillo's 167 wartime goals had also come at the wrong time. They simply didn't count and would go unheeded by the record books. And worse still! Since the current season had started with the war still in progress, the Victory League Cup – the Don's first ever national prize – would also not feature in the official records.

But all this disillusionment was yet to come. Leaving the mean, dingy tenements behind, they soon retraced their steps back over the Clyde to arrive tired but triumphant, just in time for the bus. Quizzed, they explained where they had been.

"God Almighty!" exploded Alex Brown, laughing aloud. "Ye're nae feart you twa! Ye've been touring the Gorbals!"

Shepy had certainly heard of the Gorbals and No Mean City, but it never occurred to him that there was any danger. Despite squalid slums and unmistakable privation they'd met with no menace or threat, real or imagined, in that much maligned district.

Perhaps they had been lucky. Luckier than Jock Pattillo.

"Fit's the name o' this aul street?"

Fit to print?

Heavier deliveries were made by Blair's son Alex,
an ex-p.o.w. of the Japs, in his sporty red MG

MANOEUVRING the unwieldy roll of linoleum downstairs, Shepy eventually emerged from the premises of James Blair, out into the warm sunshine in Market Street. His mission? To return the lino to house furnishers Chivas in Victoria Road and bring back a replacement roll.

As he drew level with W.&W. Lindsay, just down the street, a stocky-built, fair-haired lad arranging parcels in the basket of his bike, straightened up. His bland nod was acknowledged in similar vein by Shepy. After all, they were message boys for competing printers.

The rivalry went deeper. Only that morning, stomaching the powerful aromas emanating from Laing's People's Cafe in the market hall – enticingly appetising when homeward bound but strangely nauseating on return – something else caused his disaffection.

It was handsome Harry, leaning across his bike outside Blairs, beaming all over and chatting up Daisy, Marie, Dorothy and Isobel – practically their entire talent population.

Why couldn't the so-and-so be content making eyes at the girls in Lindsays? Shepy crossed Hadden Street when, to his immense relief, the jaunty youth gave the girls a wave and free-wheeled down the pavement to his own place of work.

And deeper yet! Playing for youth team Caley Thistle, nursery for City Boys League club Caledonian, Shepy was promoted for the match with top-rated St Clements. He clashed with Harry who shone, scoring a couple of goals with some powerful shooting.

Going upstairs with the girls, Shepy winced at their small-talk. "He telt me to ca canny on the dance fleer," giggled Daisy. "He said his feet was his fortune." Isobel sighed enamoured, "Oh, he is nice though. Isn't he?" Shepy had to admit that Lindsay's message boy had style.

Brought to earth with the cumbrous roll of linoleum and his bus fare from old man Blair, Shepy was hard-pressed to feel other than inelegant. There was no message bike. He made deliveries on foot, by bus or tram.

Heavier deliveries were made by Blair's son Alex, an ex-p.o.w. of the Japs, in his sporty red MG. Taken along to do any carrying, Shepy was enthralled by visits to HM Theatre to deliver the programmes and tickets printed by Blairs and the Palais de Danse, where Alex talked business over coffee with proprietor Ernest Bromberg and Shepy enjoyed a fruit crush – a treat now that he no longer worked at Hay's.

With spry, jocular but experienced printer Jimmy Donald and recently demobbed young Gordon Highlander Doug Shirran, Blair's machine room was fairly adequately manned. Of the former caseroom duo, both serving airmen, young Jim Campbell, however, had still to be demobbed.

In the meantime, the indefatigable Dave Young, often at the expense of his health, worked Blair's caseroom single-handed. Trade union rules allowed no apprentice unless two journeymen were employed. When that day dawned Shepy could put to professional use his expertise with the rubber type, blocking stamp and ink pad of his trusty John Bull juvenile printing outfit!

The previous message boy had unwittingly done Shepy a good turn, salvaging (as he thought), H.M. Theatre ticket "spoils" from the waste bin, he calmly occupied those seats in the parterre stalls with his pals. When the genuine ticket holders arrived, his scam was uncovered.

Blairs had to do a bit of apologising and the doltish miscreant got the boot.

With less culpability, perhaps, Shepy pocketed the fare money and walked to Torry, reckoning the roll of lino far too cumbersome to get on and off a bus.

This sort of task was a bit off-putting for a budding compositor. Blair's didn't have a Linotype machine and had big jobs typeset by the Journal's jobbing department. He didn't mind ferrying galleys of linotype from Broad Street. Lead slugs were heavy, but it was all in the cause of print. He felt tempted to put a note on the notice board: "Linotype, yes! Linoleum, no!" But he didn't have the nerve.

Perspiring freely by the time he returned to Blairs with the fresh roll of lino, the cordial office team Millie and Mabel, female equivalents of Laurel and Hardy, were waiting with news for him.

"You'll be glad to hear that Jim Campbell has been demobbed from the RAF," clucked large as life Millie.

"And that means you'll be able to start serving your time any day now," chirped dainty wee Mabel.

In the midst of the congratulations, the ever droll Jimmy Donald caught his arm. "I hear yer mate Harry next door has signed for the Dons."

"Gee!" gulped Shepy, marvelling at the news and digesting it slowly. Like many youngsters, he too dreamt of becoming a real footballer ... sometime ... someday. But it couldn't do any harm getting a good trade behind him in the interim. A voice in his ear ended his musings. It was old man Blair.

"Now I want ye tae tak' the new lino up tae the hoose in Fountainhall." adding generously, "and ye dinna need tae come back till aifter the denner hoor."

Shepy gritted his teeth. He took a great shuddering breath, raised his head and hoisted the lino on to his shoulder. His apprenticeship hadn't begun yet!

Best boot forward

He kept his eye on the ball and brought up his right foot behind him

"NOO, jist between oorsels ye ken," Bill Beedie confided, lightly slapping Shepy's thigh, signifying the end of the treatment session, "fit wid ye say tae a pair o' Alan Morton boots?"

Shepy's eyes popped. Although the event had taken place before he was born, he had heard of the famous, diminutive Rangers winger, known as "the wee blue devil", and his hallowed place among the Wembley Wizards.

Three times in that classic international encounter he had floated the ball into the English goalmouth, and three times former Don, Alex Jackson (Huddersfield), had slotted them home. Two more goals from ex-Raith Rovers star Alex James (Arsenal) added up to a dazzling 5-1 victory for Scotland at Wembley.

"He was the finest left-winger in football," extolled Bill, "and he was really right-footed."

That went down well with Shepy, himself right-footed, but preferring to play on the left. He had read somewhere of the wisdom in keeping one's stronger foot to the inside of the field rather than be limited to the narrow confines of the touch-line.

"Gee, gosh," breathed Shepy. "Well I certainly widna' say no."

"There is one proviso," said Bill, "and I suppose you can guess what that is."

Smelling of liniment and oil, Shepy slid down off the couch nodding glumly. He knew all right.

It certainly wasn't a fixture to write home about – Saints versus Victoria Utd. Just a routine juvenile league match where Shepy fully expected Saints to coast to victory. How wrong he was.

Early in the game a free kick was given against Saints, just outside the penalty area. Shepy edged back to join the line-up to block the attempt at goal. The player taking the kick thumped the ball for all he was worth and Shepy's right knee-cap caught the full force of the shot. He went down like a log, in excruciating pain.

Coach Bill Beedie and trainer Bob Sutherland ran on to the pitch. After going through the usual routine, the magic sponge alas failed to live up to its reputation. They had to carry Shepy to the touch-line, where cold compresses and bandages were applied to the swelling and he was made as comfortable as possible.

"You'll be OK," Bill assured him and promised to give him a run home after the game.

"At's the price o' ye!" bawled committee man Big Ben impatiently. "If ye wid jist bide oot on the wing like a'body keeps telling ye!"

The outburst stunned everyone in the vicinity – not least its target, the crippled Shepy.

"Jist gie him a dose o' paying nae attention," comforted Bill.

Substitutes had not yet been invented, so a miserable Shepy watched his ten colleagues fight valiantly, but in the end having to accept a one-all draw with a delighted United.

After the proceedings Shepy got a run home in Bill's wee Austin Seven, promising to attend the modest clinic set up in his Chestnut Row home. Here he treated sprained ankles, torn ligaments and numerous other football injuries as best he could, both for his own and other minor clubs.

It was Shepy's first nasty football injury and Bill maintained that rest and time were the best healers. He could only help the process along. At home Shepy's father told him to look on the bright side.

"It could've been worse if he'd aimed a bittie higher."

By Shepy's second visit Bill was regaling his captive audience with albums of team photographs and action pictures of his own footballing career with Glasgow Rangers, when he was understudy to the great Alan Morton. In prints of social occasions Bill, Alan Morton and team-mates were pictured getting in and out of taxis, trains and the team bus and on golf outings, with one engaging print featuring the two men with arms locked around each others' shoulders.

Bill kept advising Shepy to play on the wing, stressing that he didn't have the build for a wing-half. But Shepy had little enthusiasm for standing out on the wing waiting for the ball. He had to be involved in the thick of things.

It was his fourth and final session when the Alan Morton boots were produced. As Bill handed them over, he reminded Shepy of his undertaking to persevere and stick it out on the wing. Shepy was already cherishing the boots, intending to grease them with dubbin, polish and shine them, but never dare wear them.

When he got home he had just missed his father who had left for work on his 9pm to 6am shift. And he missed him the following morning when his father was asleep as he left for school. He knew his father would be impressed because he often spoke of Morton as being his boyhood hero.

At school it was, "Fa's Alan Morton onywye?" when he proudly showed off the boots, naming the player to all who would look and listen. Only Stan Blackwell, whose father had kept goal for the Dons, and Kenny Thomson, the school team's skipper, had heard of him.

When eventually he flourished them proudly before his father, who gave them a quick look over, he was crestfallen by the observations of his discerning parent.

"Alan Morton could niver play in 'at boots," he scoffed.

"Fit wye nae?" asked Shepy.

"Weel fer a start, he was a very wee fella, only 5ft. 4 ins. tall, and weighing 9 stone."

"So what!" countered Shepy.

"Well these boots are size 9 and he widna've bin ca'd the wee blue devil' wi' size 9 boots! Case closed."

Shepy groaned. "But he said they were Alan Morton's boots."

"Fa said?" asked his father.

Shepy explained to his father the link between Alan Morton and Bill.

"Oh ay, I min' him," recalled his father. "He wis an Aberdeen loon. Efter a couple o' seasons wi' Rangers, he moved to Clyde."

"Wis he a good player?" asked Shepy.

"Nae bad. But he didna mak' the first team breakthrough. Plenty ither clubs were efter him though."

"You telt me they were Alan Morton's boots," sulked Shepy on their next meeting. Bill shook his head. "Na. Fit I said wis they were Alan Morton boots. Ye ken fit I mean – the same make and brand as he wore. I niver said they were his boots." Rather sheepishly he admitted, "They were actually my ain boots. I've got anither pair."

In the circumstances, Shepy reckoned the boots were devalued, being only the boots of Alan Morton's deputy. This was not quite the same thing, so he decided to make practical use of them in his next outing.

This he did, also requiring a knee bandage and extra socks to fill out the boots. The match was against the unbeaten Waterton, a very formidable side.

It was some time before Shepy, out on the wing, wonky knee and all, gained possession. Dummying the wing-half, he confidently nudged the ball along with the outside of his boot as he dribbled up the wing, challenging the stocky right-back cannily approaching. Poised to flick the ball past the back, Shepy was not expecting the hefty tackle that followed. The defender made a wild scything lunge, sweeping his feet from under him with aplomb, consummately removing him from the field of play, and then had the nerve to claim the throw-in.

"Oh no. Nae again," wailed Big Ben. But once more Shepy was carried to the touch-line. His bootlaces were loosened and cold water poured on both ankles before he returned to the fray, limping badly.

There were only minutes left when Saints attacking centre-half Sonny Adams burst through on the right wing, outpacing the full-back and getting behind the Waterton defence. With his wonky knee and dodgy ankles Shepy hirpled into the middle for the anticipated cross.

Perhaps his boots had not been laced up properly after his spill, but as he struggled to meet a waist-high cross-ball, the studs of one boot somehow got caught in the laces of the other boot and he sprawled forward on his hands.

As he tumbled headlong, however, he kept his eye on the ball and brought up his right foot behind him, performing what could only be termed an overhead back-heeler, catapulting the ball into the net, beating the bemused keeper all ends up.

It was the only goal of the game – struck by the heel of the boot of the man who was Alan Morton's stand-in.

Bill Beedie, the Saint's coach, had been an able deputy for the great Alan Morton and a fine winger with Clyde. This doyen of the game did his damnedest to lead Shepy along the same path. Perhaps Shepy should have listened to him.

Jake's Record Finish

> "*Now listen all you sinners,*
> *If you want to get to heaven ....*"

Old Jake Shepherd was off work and, in his neat Leadside flat, was carrying out an inventory of all his possessions. The "Sons of the Pioneers" songsters were in good fettle as he played old favourites on the time-worn portable gramophone he persisted in calling his phonograph, whilst taking the opportunity to clear out obsolete articles, clothes and paraphernalia gradually accumulated over the years and including the dish, brush, collar leash, etc., left untouched since the death of his beloved Scotch terrier.

Various ornaments and bits and pieces were earmarked for particular friends and relatives. But Jake was in no doubt about who would appreciate the ancient Monarch table gramophone, complete with brass horn, and blaring away atop the little dresser.

> "*Get down on your knees and pray.*
> *Make ready for judgement day.*
> *Open up them pearly gates for me.*
> *Hallelujah, lujah!*"

A more modest project was under way just around the square at Shepy's home. His dad, now demobbed and back portering at the hospital, was clearing out his overflowing drawer in the sideboard, just marking time until the arrival of a van from Smart Bros. in St Nicholas Street with a brand new-fangled radiogram to replace the old HMV mahogany, wind-up cabinet gramophone, being taken in part payment.

He knew full well that if he attempted anything of this nature while Shepy was in the vicinity, he would finish up shifting articles from one place to another and getting rid of nothing. However, being on the 12 noon to 9pm shift, he was uninterrupted during the entire forenoon, as he tore up old letters, postcards and bills, threw out magazines, cricket and football fixture almanacs and, the hardest task of the lot, giving up a collection of treasured paperbacks, including "The Grapes of Wrath", "A World I Never Made" and "The Jungle".

Old Jake was not in perfect health, and the death of his dog hadn't helped. Shepy had visited him a couple of times recently along with his dad. Off his own bat on this occasion, however, he decided to pay a visit during his lunch hour, his dad well away to work by then.

Shepy had not forgotten how, in earlier years, Jake had allowed him and his pals the freedom of the mill in Jack's Brae during the quiet evenings, provided they caused no damage. And how, when they had exhausted themselves playing every action game you could imagine, he would enthrall them with slightly embroidered stories from the First World War.

After Shepy had respectfully enquired about Jake's health and expressed sympathy about the loss of his dog, the old-timer smiled.

"Dinna worry. Fan I get to the gates of heaven that dog will be waiting for me." His kindly eyes seemed to search Shepy's as he continued. "Now foo wid ye like my phonograph?"

Shepy was struck dumb – an unusual affliction for him – and the old man's face lit up like a child's. Without more ado he proceeded to show a still dazed Shepy how to operate the record player, using the ubiquitous disc "Pearly Gates", the swansong significance of which, to all intents and purposes, was lost upon the excited Shepy.

Later, dismantling the horn, Jake carefully closed the case. He patted Shepy on the head, giving him a box of needles and a ten bob note.

With a bit of a struggle, horn under his left arm, case handle in his right hand, Shepy managed to carry the apparatus from Leadside to his home nearby.

"Dis yer da ken aboot this?" asked his mother, receiving only a vague nod in reply.

Four hours later, heading home from work, Shepy decided to get some reading matter for the weekend and made his way to Broadfoot's second-hand bookshop on Woolmanhill.

Browsing around the shelves his eyes lit on a Penguin edition of "Beau Geste". He had enjoyed the film, so he picked up the book. Just then he noticed books nearby – Upton Sinclair, John Steinbeck and James T. Farrell, authors he was certain would please his father. Jake's ten shilling note was put to use without hesitation.

It was the following day before Shepy's father found out about the gramophone his son had been given by Jake, and he was none too pleased. Expecting his new radiogram any day, he didn't want a machine in the house that was even more of a relic than the one he was trading in.

"So faur aboot in the hoose dae ye think that's gaun?" he asked in despair. "Ye had nae business takin' it in onywye withoot asking me first."

"Now foo wid ye like my phonograph?"

But that was not all!

When presented with the books Shepy had bought, hoping they would impress him, he nearly exploded. His eyes shot heavenwards for strength as it became evident they were part of the collection he himself had deposited at Broadfoot's the previous day – unbeknown to Shepy.

But, seeing Shepy's expression of utter dejection, he began to relent, saying he could keep the antique gramophone in the meantime. As to the books, he now saw the unwitting, comical cross-purposes of the affair and grinned.

"Thanks, really. I thocht a lot o' those books onywye. Fa kens? Could be I wis mint to haud on tae them for a bittie langer."

Almost a month went by. Then one day Shepy learned from his father that old Jake had died peacefully. Tears welled up in his eyes at the news and he was plunged into gloom.

"Cheer up," consoled his mother. "He will get his reward in heaven."

Shepy wavered. "Ay, but is there really a heaven?"

"Weel if there's nae," moralised his father, "then there should be for folk like Jake!"

Benumbed, Shepy went through to the little bedroom, set up the old gramophone and put on a brightly-labelled record. It was the one Jake played on his last visit. He began to think ...

Jake must have suspected his days were numbered, and this was his goodbye record. Fighting back the tears, he now felt deeply that Jake was some man, and he would never see him again, well ... God willing?

> "*When you hear that trumpet blast,*
> *I'll be coming home at last.*
> *Open up them pearly gates for me.*"

Jake had gone for good. Shepy was growing up and his nickname soon petered out. They say a good nickname will wear out, but a bad one may last forever. It was the end of an era and perhaps fitting that it just die a natural death.

Glossary

Aboot about
Affa awful
Ahin behind
Aifter after
Ain own
Aince once
Aleen alone
Ane one
Aneith beneath
A'thin everything
Auld old
Ava at all
Awa away

Backet bucket
Bairn child
Beau geste gallant gesture
Bide stay
Biler boiler
Bocht bought
Boord board
Brak break
Breest breast
Broon brown

Ca canny go safely
Canna cannot
Coont count
Craitur creature

Dae do
Deen done
Dinna do not
Disna doesn't
Doon down
Doot doubt
Doup bottom
Droont drowned

Eerans errands
Eese use
Fa who
Fae from
Fan when
Faur where
Fear't afraid
Feel fool
Fit what, foot
Fitiver whatever
Fit's adee what's wrong
Fleer floor
Foo how
Fustlin whistling

Gang, ging go
Gar to make, cause
Gart made
Gie give
Gin if
Gollach creepy-crawly
Greet weep
G'wa go away
Gweed good
Gyaun going
Gypit stupid

Haiverin' foolish
Hale whole
Hame home
Haud hold
Heid head
Hid had
Hing hang
Hinnered hindered
Hiv have
Hunners hundreds

Jist just

Ken know

Lang long
Lat let
Licht light

Loon boy
Lum chimney

Mak make
Maik half-penny
Mair more
Maistly mostly
Maitter matter
Masel myself
Maun must
Micht might
Muckle much

Nae not
Naebody nobody
Naethin' nothing
Nesty nasty
Neep turnip
Nivver never
Noo now

Ony any
Onywye anyway
Oot out
Ower too, over

Pit put
Pucklie some
Pudden dunce

Ragged teased
Richt right
Rinnin' running
Roon round
Rumblin' rumbling

Sair sore
Scudding strapping
Shargart stunted
Siller money
Sine since
Skelpit smacked
Sotter mess
Spleet split, brand
Spikkin' speaking
Stane stone
Staun stand
Steer stir
Stumor bad choice
Sunkies cellars

Tatties potatoes
Taen taken
Teir tear
Telt told
Thocht thought
Toon town
Toonsers town folk
Twa two

Vantas mineral water

Waur worse
Weel well
Weer wear
Wheesht hush
Widna would not
Wight wager
Winna will not
Wis was
Worsit wool
Wrang wrong
Wye way
Wypers Ypres

Ye you
Yoket get started